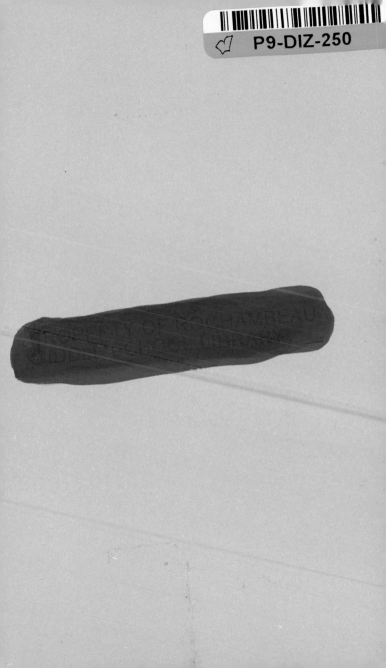

P9-DIZ-250

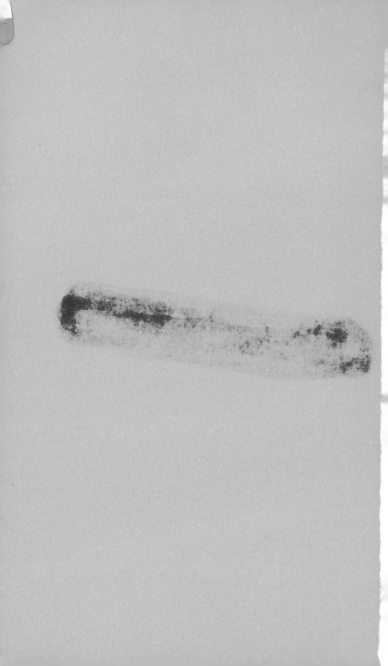

LETTERS
from the
MOUNTAIN

OTHER BOOKS BY SHERRY GARLAND

Song of the Buffalo Boy

The Silent Storm

The Lotus Seed
Illustrated by Tatsuro Kiuchi

Shadow of the Dragon

Indio

The Summer Sands
Illustrated by Robert J. Lee

Cabin 102

LETTERS
from the
MOUNTAIN

SHERRY GARLAND

Harcourt Brace & Company

San Diego   New York   London

Requests for permission to make copies of any part of the work should
be mailed to: Permissions Department, Harcourt Brace & Company,
6277 Sea Harbor Drive, Orlando, Florida 32887-6777.

Library of Congress Cataloging-in-Publication Data
Garland, Sherry.
Letters from the mountain/Sherry Garland.—1st ed.
p.   cm.
Summary: A teenage boy, sent for the summer to relatives in the
mountains in order to remove him from gang influences, discovers
life's really important values through his unlikely friendship with
an economically challenged boy.
ISBN 0-15-200661-3   0-15-200659-1 (pbk.)
[1. Mountain life—Fiction. 2. Gangs—Fiction. 3. Friendship—
Fiction.] I. Title.
PZ7.G18415Le   1996
[Fic]—dc20   96-2257

Text set in Granjon
Designed by Lydia D'moch
First edition
A B C D E
A B C D E (pbk.)
Printed in Hong Kong

*To the librarians and teachers
of Nacogdoches, Texas—
Thanks, Zoe-Linda,
for lending me your name*

LETTERS
from the
MOUNTAIN

1

To Whom It May Concern:

I killed DeWayne Lockhart and this is how it happened.

DeWayne was this motormouth kid that lived down the street from me. He didn't have any friends because of his big mouth and weird-looking hair that stuck up in every which way. But this DeWayne guy took a liking to me, I don't know why, I guess maybe because one day on the bus I let him sit next to me because Packer had skipped school that day and I'd been saving it for him. DeWayne wouldn't leave me alone after that. He'd give me his dessert at lunch and was always giving me money for video games. I didn't ask for it, he just did it.

When DeWayne found out I belonged to a friendly little group of guys called the Northside Lynch Mob, he started begging to join.

I didn't want to be rude, but this was

my gang of friends—Jeremy, Packer, and the Spencer brothers, Eric and Errol. Five was the perfect number and, besides, Jeremy wouldn't want a weirdo like DeWayne in the gang.

Anyway, this DeWayne guy kept following me around and showing up at my house, and my mom, the once or twice she was home, said, "He seems nice. Let him in and give him a Coke, for Pete's sake." She said he had the best manners of any of my friends and wished I had more like him. It made me want to puke.

Jeremy started getting pretty upset because DeWayne found out where we had our secret meetings—down under the bayou bridge about three blocks from the apartments where I live. We did as we pleased down there with no interruptions—except for DeWayne. Jeremy told me if I didn't start controlling DeWayne, I was out of the Lynch Mob. Jeremy was our leader. We never had an election or anything like that, he just was. He didn't live in the apartments like me and Packer and the Spencer brothers. Jeremy lived in a cool house with a pool in the back, but he never used it. He liked hanging with us better and doing risky stuff like snitching candy bars from the Stop-n-Go or tagging buildings with spray paint.

It was my suggestion that we get rid of DeWayne by making him go through some kind of humiliating initiation. What I had in mind was to tell him that every member had to stand stark naked in front of the Stop-n-Go, or something stupid like that. I knew DeWayne would balk. Jeremy liked my idea of initiation, but not the naked part.

He told DeWayne he had to go through three tests. The first one was to snitch a candy bar from the Stop-n-Go. DeWayne was so clumsy and goofy, we figured he'd get caught right away, but he didn't. He'd been in there dozens of times and was the honest type and the clerk liked him, so he never even glanced DeWayne's way.

Next, Jeremy told DeWayne he'd have to snitch a can of spray paint from the hardware store. DeWayne not only did it, he did it when his father was shopping for a socket set! Put it right in the basket and told his dad it was for a school project. It sat there right up till the minute before paying for it. DeWayne just told his dad he was going to put it back, but slipped it under his shirt instead.

I thought that was pretty cool and was beginning to think maybe DeWayne wasn't so bad after all. He had nerves of steel, doing all the tests without blinking twice. But Jeremy was spitting mad because goofy DeWayne was accomplishing things that Jeremy and the rest of us had to learn the hard way. With DeWayne looking all geeky and average-like, it was putting Jeremy to shame.

Jeremy must have been really ticked off and that's why he set the next initiation as something really risky. He met us under the bridge with a can of paint remover he'd swiped from his stepdad and said, "Here's the solution to the DeWayne problem. One snort of this stuff and he'll be history."

Me and Packer saw the skull and crossbones on the can and said something like "Won't this kill him?" but Jeremy said, "Naw, I've huffed it a few times. It just makes your head go all crazy, then you puke your guts out."

When DeWayne met us and saw the can and the plastic bag, he asked if we'd done it and was it dangerous, and we all lied and said yes, we'd done it. I felt bad, and almost told Jeremy to stop, but I guess I was mad at DeWayne, too, for showing us up and being so nerdy. Why couldn't he have just been normal?

DeWayne breathed the fumes, got a goofy look on his face, then sorta floated to the ground and went into convulsions. After that he got all still.

I shook DeWayne, but he didn't move. Jeremy's face was as white as a sheet, and he told us to get out of there fast. I wanted to go for help, but Jeremy said we would all end up in the state pen for life, so we scrambled up the banks of the levee like scared rabbits. We ran and ran and ran. I never ran so hard in my life. Jeremy made us all swear to never tell a living soul, and we did the special Lynch Mob handgrip—all five of our hands were shaking as they touched and it reminded me of coming out of a huddle in a football game, only this was no game.

I was supposed to go straight home and pretend nothing happened, but I had to cross the bayou bridge to get there, and when I did I saw DeWayne so still and cold looking, I couldn't help myself. I ran to the phone booth at the Stop-n-Go and called 911. I didn't even have to disguise my voice, because it was all squeaky and shaky and nobody would have recognized it. I hid behind a trash dumpster and waited for the ambulance. The smell made me sick at my stomach. I saw two teenage girls walking down the levee. All heck broke loose when they stumbled onto DeWayne. They ran like maniacs to the store and told the owner. By the time he got there, the ambulance had arrived. I watched and shook like a leaf from head to toe until the medics had loaded DeWayne on the stretcher and the ambulance's red light had vanished down the street. Then I puked on the sidewalk.

I heard on the news that night that DeWayne was in a coma. The TV showed his parents: His father had glasses and weird hair and his mother had a goofy mouth just like DeWayne. They were crying.

The next day I saw a police car out in front of the apartments and my heart nearly stopped. I was sure someone had seen us with DeWayne, but it was something else. The Stop-n-Go owner had seen Packer snitching batteries and stuff and was pressing charges. Packer was two years older than me—fifteen. He was dumb as nails and had flunked twice and had to go to summer school every year, but he was a good friend and always had the highest scores on Mortal Kombat. We called him Packer because he always packed everything but the kitchen sink in his big pockets. Poor guy, it was his fifth offense. Nobody could save him this time and his dad didn't care, so Packer was sent to juvenile detention.

The day after the accident, I called Jeremy and said maybe we should tell somebody what happened, but he said he'd kick my butt if I squealed. He called me a mama's boy on account of I don't have a dad and live with my mom, and he called me a sissy and 'fraidy-cat and lots of other things, too. Then he reminded me about the time he'd lied for me when I got caught tagging the back wall of Ernie's Motors. That was the time Jeremy told the police he saw two Lobo gang members running down the road with spray cans.

Jeremy was always covering for me like that; he was more like a big brother than our leader and always did what it took to keep us together. He made up this oath that we all swore to uphold. It goes like this: "Northside Lynch Mob is my true family, my only family. I swear to protect friends before family, before myself. Northside Lynch Mob Rules Forever!" He even taught us a secret handshake and secret signals that no one else knows. And every time one of us got into trouble, he would give the secret signal and say, "Friends before Family." He called it our motto.

After Jeremy's lecture to me about what a cowardly traitor I would be to the Lynch Mob, I kept my mouth shut. Then he told me he was spending the summer with his real dad in Arizona, where he could lay low until things cooled off.

Packer's gone, Jeremy's gone, and the Spencer brothers got summer jobs with Tony's Lawn Service, so I don't have anyone to talk to and it gets really lonely and boring. Last night, the news said DeWayne is still in a coma and may not live. I've made up my mind about something. If you're reading this letter, it means that DeWayne Lockhart died and I just couldn't take it any longer. I'm sorry for what I did.

> Sincerely,
> Taylor D. Ryan

Taylor folded the sheets of notebook paper and stuffed them into an envelope. He licked and sealed it, then scribbled "To be opened upon the death of Taylor D. Ryan" across the front. He looked around his room, from the Bruce Lee posters on one wall to the pile of dirty clothes in the corner. After studying all possibilities, he rolled the envelope into a cylinder and shoved it inside the body of an old model airplane that had been hanging from the ceiling as long as he could remember. He thought it had belonged to his dad but wasn't sure.

He examined the airplane from different angles until he was sure that no part of the letter was showing.

A light rapping sounded at his door, startling him.

"Taylor, have you packed your clothes?" His mother's voice came through the closed door.

Taylor gritted his teeth, then jumped up

from the bed to check the lock on his door. He pressed his ear to the wood and held his breath.

"Taylor, I know you're in there. If you don't pack your clothes, then I will. And you know how that will turn out. Taylor?"

A smile crept to Taylor's lips when he saw the doorknob move slightly then stop. Let her wonder if he was still alive, it would serve her right for what she was about to do to him.

"You'll like it on the mountain. It's beautiful up there." She paused. "It's for your own good, Taylor, dear." She rattled the doorknob again, then sighed.

"Okay, fine. Be stubborn as usual, but you're still going." Cold steel suddenly edged her voice and Taylor swallowed hard.

He listened to her footsteps fade away and heard the bathroom door slam. All his mom had done for the past year was yell and slam doors and treat him like a little kid. And all he did was keep his mouth shut and sneak out every chance he got. If it hadn't been for Jeremy and the Lynch Mob, Taylor wouldn't have spoken more than a dozen words a day. He tried to tell his mom once how cool Jeremy and Packer were, but she flew into a rage about hoodlums and drugs and guns. One night she even nailed a board over the bedroom window and propped a chair in front of his door so he wouldn't go out. But it didn't do any good, he sneaked out anyway and spent that night hidden in Eric and Errol's closet. After that, he didn't even try to talk to his mother anymore, and she didn't talk to him, either.

Taylor turned out his lights and crawled into bed. The neon sign of an all-night Texaco station blinked outside his window. It was hot but the air conditioner wasn't on and the window was up because his mom wanted to save on the electric bill. Cars and trucks buzzed by like angry hornets and a few streets over a siren howled. The odor of exhaust fumes and garbage drifted into the dark room.

Taylor closed his eyes, but he could not sleep.

2

The hot, dry wind of June brought down the smell of cedar from the mountains. It stirred up white dust and layered it over the tops of cars and pickups in the graveled parking lot in front of Boyd's Café and Gas Station.

Taylor Ryan sat on the Greyhound bus bench watching the white dust swirl and thinking about DeWayne. It had been a whole week since the accident, and still he could not get DeWayne out of his mind. But it wasn't the old annoying DeWayne, the one *before* the accident, that Taylor was thinking about. It was the new DeWayne, the one *after* the accident, that was consuming his thoughts. DeWayne lying on the green bank of the bayou foaming at the mouth, DeWayne jerking in uncontrollable convulsions, DeWayne suddenly very limp and still.

A noisy bus squealed to a halt in front of Taylor, sending a blast of hot, oily fumes into his face. He ran his fingers through his dark, curly hair and kicked his duffel bag out of the way of some unloading passengers. He counted five people stepping off, not including the baby in one woman's arms.

Why on earth would five grown adults want to come to Pandora, Texas? Taylor thought. The whole population must have just gone up one whole percentile with their arrival. From the way they were talking and smiling, they were kin to each other. Probably going to some kind of family reunion.

A little sigh escaped from Taylor's lips. That was one thing he would never have to worry about—a big family reunion. He could count his family members on the fingers of his left hand, and most of those he'd never even met. But that was going to change in a few minutes, thanks to his mother's latest brainstorm.

It's for your own good, Taylor, dear. Those had been her parting words. Not *I'll miss you, Taylor, dear,* or *Be careful up on that mountain, Taylor, dear,* or *Hurry home soon, Taylor, dear.*

Taylor liked his mother better when she was honest, even if it meant she was boiling mad. All the while she had driven him to the bus station in Houston early that morning, he kept expecting her to confess she was sending him to the top of a forsaken mountain to keep him out of her hair for the summer. Or to keep him away from his friends. He expected her to lash out with her angry tongue like she did the time he got caught snitching radio batteries, saying things like *You've got a police record now, thanks to those bad friends,* or *I warned you to stay away from those bad friends,* or *You're ruining your life because of those bad friends.*

Bad friends. That was what his mother always called the little group he hung out with. She didn't know they called themselves the Northside Lynch Mob. Jeremy had thought up that name because it sounded so deadly, but Taylor didn't think of the Lynch Mob as a real gang, not like the kind in the rougher parts of the city—the kind who stole cars and robbed houses and snorted dope and had drive-by shootings. All the Lynch Mob did was get together after school and mess around. Maybe snitch a candy bar or two from the Stop-n-Go, maybe swipe a can of spray paint now and then and tag an old abandoned wall. At least they didn't paint on the backs of people's houses or cars or important places like that. Nothing serious. No drugs.

Wham! An image slammed into Taylor's brain like an exploding bullet. It was DeWayne opening a can of paint remover and letting the fumes ease into a plastic bag, giggling nervously as he placed his face into the bag and huffed. His round blue eyes had grown rounder behind his metal-rimmed glasses and for a moment they seemed to glow. He huffed again, and then very gently took the bag away and made that goofy smile that only DeWayne could make. *Cool,* he said to Taylor just before his eyes rolled back and he collapsed onto the green grass. That's when he started the convulsions. And then silence as his face turned the color of day-old ashes in a fireplace.

But that wasn't the worst of it. It was the running away afterward that made a sour taste rise from Taylor's stomach. He put his hands over his ears and rocked back and forth as he tried to block out the memories pounding on his skull, demanding to be recognized.

"Stop it! Stop! Leave me alone!" Taylor yelled, as if the memory were a living, breathing person standing in front of him. He jumped up and paced around and around the bench, pausing to kick his duffel bag every time he passed it. The gas-station attendant looked at him like he was crazy, then returned to his magazine.

Maybe he'd be crazy, too, if he had a memory that wouldn't leave him in peace, Taylor thought.

A memory that chased him down like hounds after a fox. Every hour, every second of the day banging on his brain.

After a few minutes Taylor felt exhausted, so he bought a Dr. Pepper from the soft-drink machine and pressed the cold can against his forehead. The condensation dribbled down his cheek and neck, blending with the beads of sweat. A banged-up Coca-Cola thermometer on the outside wall registered ninety degrees, and the reek of manure from an empty eighteen-wheeler cattle truck parked at the café occasionally drifted to the gas station.

Taylor had just finished off the soft drink and sat back down when an old blue-and-white Buick Special pulled to a halt in front of the bench. A small woman with startling white hair and a peaches-and-cream complexion smiled from the passenger seat, while a tall man wearing a white Western hat stepped out of the driver's side.

"You must be Taylor," the man said and rushed to pick up the duffel bag. His knees cracked loudly as he stooped over. He was tanned and slim, except for a little soft belly that pushed out against his blue denim overalls.

"I'm Earl Butler, your grandpa's brother," the man said as he opened the car trunk. "Just call me Uncle Earl. And that's your Aunt Etta."

"How'do," the woman said. Her gray eyes twinkled as she watched Taylor settle into the clean backseat.

"I do believe you are the spitting image of your father," Earl said as he slid behind the driver's wheel. "Look at that chin and jawline and—"

"Oh, don't be an old fool!" Aunt Etta interrupted him, her head twisted around like an owl's, staring at Taylor. "You'd have to be blind not to see that he's the spitting image of his mother. Those eyes are the same hazel-green color."

Taylor winced. The last person in the world he wanted to look like was his mom. Those hazel eyes narrowed down to green catlike slits when she got mad at him. And for the last year everything he did turned her into a screaming harpy with long red nails. *Your room looks like a pigsty! Don't play that music so loud, I'm trying to sleep! Don't stay out so late! You'd better do your homework or you'll flunk the seventh grade! Why don't you act your age for a while! It's those bad boys you hang out with, they're ruining your life!*

Taylor leaned back into the seat as the Buick

sped down the deserted two-lane county road and tried to block out the sound of the old couple bickering. They apparently knew every human in the county, both living and dead, and made a point of telling Taylor details of every scandal, murder, or tragedy that had happened in the past hundred years. Cemeteries were in great supply and Butlers seemed to be planted under every live oak, though Taylor didn't see more than a handful of living people.

Cows and horses grazed lazily in most of the pastures. In one large field a hay baler smoked and rumbled, spitting out neat golden rectangles of wired hay. Teenage boys, stripped to their waists and tanned, lifted the bales onto the back of a flatbed truck. Their muscles rippled and reminded Taylor of the weight-lifting equipment that Jeremy's stepfather bought him for his fifteenth birthday. The Lynch Mob lifted weights all summer, then went to the mall and bought matching muscle shirts and paraded up and down Galveston beach trying to impress the girls. Jeremy was always coming up with ideas like that and always had the money to do it.

The Buick rumbled past a few old farmhouses surrounded by fields of green plants, some covered with yellow blooms, others heavy with heads of green seed. As far as Taylor could see, the plants stood at attention in rows.

"Farley's cotton looks good," Uncle Earl commented.

"His sorghum's getting a late start," Aunt Etta replied.

"No it ain't. Looks fine."

Another round of bickering began. Taylor closed his eyes. Now he knew where his mom got her arguing ways. This was going to be even worse than he had imagined. In spite of all the times he had complained about his mom not understanding him, he had to admit she knew exactly how to hurt him. Juvenile detention would have been better than the torture of staying with these two old fighting badgers all summer. Packer was in juvenile detention right now, probably watching TV or lifting weights or just sleeping. Jeremy was no doubt lounging around in his father's fancy swimming pool in Arizona, and if Taylor knew the Spencer brothers, they were probably flirting with every cute girl they saw while mowing lawns.

The sound of a blaring horn made Taylor jump out of his skin.

"What's wrong?" Taylor asked. He blinked and rubbed his eyes, unaware of how long he had been daydreaming.

The Buick had turned off the main road onto a rocky unpaved one. The gently rolling plains had turned into small mountains and steep hills covered with cedars, accentuated by rugged gray cliffs and boulders. Clumps of prickly pear cactus dotted the hillsides.

"Haney's Curve up ahead," Uncle Earl said. "Etta always gets hysterical and hits the horn every time we go around this blind curve. I've been driving these mountains for forty-five years and never used the horn."

"And I suppose old Bill Haney didn't use the horn either the day he ran head-on into that tractor," Aunt Etta remarked.

Earl muttered something under his breath and pressed the gas pedal. As the Buick leaped forward and sped around the blind curve, Taylor held his breath. His heart beat faster and he wanted to leap out the window as the gravel and dust spewed out from the tires like a volcano, leaving behind a white cloud.

"Slow down, Earl," Etta demanded. "Somebody's up ahead."

Earl grumbled a few indecipherable words as he leaned on the brakes. The Buick slid over the gravel and slowed to a crawl behind a small, dirty camper being pulled by a flatbed truck.

"See there, you almost got us killed." Etta

fanned herself furiously with a piece of junk mail.

"Might have known—it's Vernon Sinkler," Earl said, removing his hat for the first time during the past thirty minutes. Taylor was surprised to see that the gray hair sticking out from under the hat brim was only a fringe around a shiny bald head. The line where the dark tan ended and the untanned skin began contrasted as sharply as the two-tone Buick. Taylor would have snickered, except that his stomach still had butterflies from the near wreck.

"Didn't know the Sinklers were back," Aunt Etta said. "Wonder who hired him to cut posts?"

"Nobody. I imagine Vernon's out knocking on doors looking for work."

"Don't we have a few blackjacks that need thinning on the south side?"

Earl rubbed his chin. "Maybe a few. I'll check tomorrow morning."

The slow-moving contraption reminded Taylor of a wasp, with the narrow waist being the coupler between the truck and the camper. As they passed the camper, three children with hair of varying shades of red pressed their freckled faces to the windows and waved.

Sitting on the back of the flatbed truck, holding on to a spotted bird dog, was a red-headed boy who appeared to be about fourteen or fifteen. Dressed in patched denim overalls and a faded shirt, he looked like he'd never set foot in a town bigger than Pandora. His dark brown eyes stared at Taylor, the lips tight and motionless.

Earl honked the horn as the Buick passed the truck. The driver, a scrawny man with a scrawny beard, lifted one finger and nodded recognition. A small red-haired woman in the passenger's seat glanced their way but didn't smile or wave.

"Where do the Sinklers live?" Taylor asked. From the shabby looks of the boy, Taylor didn't imagine that they would have anything in common, but he was curious about the only other teen he had seen since his arrival.

Aunt Etta turned in her seat, surprise in her eyes.

"Why, the Sinklers don't live anywhere, honey. All they own is in that trailer. They're post cutters." She pronounced the words as if that was all the explanation required.

"Oh," Taylor said, then leaned back against the seat. He only looked out of the rear window once. The flatbed was inching along behind them, spewing a small white cloud over the cedar trees. The dust clinging to the trees reminded Taylor of artificial snow on Christmas trees. His mom never would buy a real one. Too messy, she said. But he'd smelled them at the grocery stores, and once Jeremy had swiped a can of fake snow. They tagged several cars in the apartment parking lot that night with the words *Merry Xmas*. Nobody appreciated their holiday spirit.

The post cutters had long been out of sight when the Buick rattled over a wooden bridge, then slowed and turned onto a gravel road at the foot of the largest mountain. A rock fence rambled in both directions, split by a high wooden entry arch with a big sign on squeaky hinges dangling from it. WELCOME TO BUTLER'S HOPE, TEXAS—FISHERMEN WELCOME.

"There she is," Earl announced proudly. "Mockingbird Mountain."

If you'd been raised in the Rockies or the Appalachians or the Smokies, you'd laugh your head off at this being called a mountain, but it looked steep enough to give the old Buick a hard time.

"I'm going to check with Lecil," Uncle Earl said, and stopped the car in front of a run-down building with the words EARL'S GENERAL STORE painted across a wooden sign out front. It was squeezed right between a small screened-in shack called EARL'S BAIT HOUSE and a dilapidated hotel called FISHERMAN'S PARADISE MOTEL. Pick-up trucks pulling boats were parked in front of two of the five tiny units. Across from the gravel road and parking area, two forlorn-looking houses on stilts nestled at the foot of the mountain. A brown-and-white beagle walked from one of them toward the car, his tail wagging.

About one hundred yards away from the store, a gristmill made of tan and white flag-stones squatted beside a little creek. Its huge wooden paddle wheel turned slowly. Farther back in the dense woods, a white rock chimney stuck out above the cedar trees, but Taylor could not tell if there was a building attached to it anymore. A cedar post corral near the mill contained a few donkeys and a small herd of Angora goats. Chickens wandered where they pleased.

A minute later, Earl returned, followed by a short, muscular man with a cigarette dangling from his lips. His apron reeked of fish and blood and some red stains that looked like bar-becue sauce. His gray hair, cropped into a very short crew cut, revealed a few tiny scars.

"Lecil, this is Taylor. Virginia's boy."

Lecil leaned toward the window until his black eyes met Taylor's.

"He's the spitting image of Ginny. Got the same hazel-green eyes and curly hair." As he stuck his hand through the window, a red-and-green-and-black dragon tattoo gleamed in the pale sunlight. Taylor shook the fishy-smelling hand reluctantly, then wiped his hand on his jeans.

Earl crawled back behind the wheel, and the Buick groaned as it climbed up the mountain, switching into second gear as it came closer to the top. Taylor nervously watched the tires creep dangerously close to gray boulders and jagged cliffs on the side of the road. One wrong move and the car would be a pile of scrap metal. With one final groan, the Buick crawled over the top and burst forward on level ground.

Cedar branches hung low, scraping the car roof as it rumbled down the twisting, narrow dirt road covered with crushed limestone rock. At last they arrived at a house made of the same flagstone as the gristmill. Hunks of petrified wood spelled out the word WELCOME above the front porch. While Earl got the duffel bag, Aunt Etta opened the front door. A black-and-white border collie barked and snarled until she was convinced that Taylor was not a threat.

The smell of chocolate cake drifted through the living room, mingling with the lingering aroma of Pine-sol. The walls, floor, and every inch of the house were spotless. Taylor imagined Aunt Etta on her hands and knees scrubbing for hours as she prepared for his visit. Too bad for her. He had no intention of staying more than one day.

"Your room is up in the attic," Aunt Etta said, "but it should be nice and cool. Earl hooked up the window fan before we left. The grandkids always fought over who would get to sleep up there at Christmas. They were convinced they could catch Santy Clause on the roof if they stayed up all night."

"Nice view of the river, too," Earl added. "We'll fix you up with a fishing rod tomorrow. You never know what you might catch in the river. I caught a thirty-pound yeller cat once after a big rain. There she was, pretty as you please, on my trotline."

Uncle Earl rattled on as he lumbered up the narrow stairs. When he reached the top, he stopped to draw in deep breaths.

"Whew, the old lungs ain't what they used to be, Etta Mae," he said with a chuckle.

"Nothing *ain't* what it used to be," she replied from the attic room where she was turning back the bedcovers. True to her word, a small window fan whirred away, making the room breezy and cool. Aunt Etta shivered and flipped it off.

"You really don't need the fan at night. A nice breeze always comes up around ten o'clock. Supper will be ready in an hour. I'll come get you then."

"I'm not hungry," Taylor said. "Just leave me alone the rest of the night, okay?"

Earl glanced at Etta, opened his mouth to speak, but she shoved him out the door. "Go on and light the oven for me, Earl."

After Earl's footsteps had faded down the creaky stairs, Etta turned to Taylor.

"I know you don't want to be here, but here you are. I told Virginia that we'd be happy to keep you all summer "

"I'm not staying." Taylor cut her short.

"Like I was saying, we don't mind. We'll provide the room and meals. All we expect from you is to help out with a few chores. Of course, Earl will pay you for any work you do at the gristmill."

Taylor groaned and plopped down on the bed. "Work? Nobody said anything to me about work."

"We'll talk about it in the morning. I'll leave your supper in the fridge in case you get hungry for a midnight snack. Sleep tight." She started to pull the door behind her, then stopped.

"One other thing, Taylor. See that little desk over there?"

Taylor didn't move. No point in cooperating with the old white-haired hag. That would just start a bad precedent.

"I bought you some writing paper, envelopes, stamps, and a new pack of ballpoints. Maybe it's the old retired schoolteacher in me, but I always find that putting my thoughts down on paper helps to work things out."

"I hate writing," Taylor protested. "In case Mom forgot to tell you, I just flunked out of English class. Grammar and junk like that is my worst subject."

"I don't care about the grammar or spelling or the contents because I will never set eyes on your letters. What I want you to do is write at least one letter a day while you're here."

Taylor got up from the bed and walked to the window. He could see the tops of cedar trees and the sun setting behind a nearby mountain. He could just make out the curve of the Brazos River, marked by shadowy rows of trees. "I ain't writing no letters." Taylor smiled to himself. There, that ought to put her school-teacher teeth on edge.

"Well, we'll see. A letter a day. To anyone you wish. If you want them mailed, put a stamp on them. If not, they won't go anywhere and you can take them home with you when you leave. Just drop each day's letter in the wicker box in the kitchen. Earl takes the mail to the box down by the general store every morning. Postman picks it up around noon."

"And I guess you'll read them and report back to my mom."

"No, I promise not to read a single line of your mail. Won't even read the addresses. You can drop them in the mailbox yourself, if you don't trust us."

After Aunt Etta left, Taylor glared at the desk. The paper was just a stack of yellow notepads, the envelopes the cheap kind you buy at a discount store. He sat down and snatched up a ballpoint pen, then jotted down a short letter addressed to his mother. That would show her exactly what he thought of her.

Dear Mom,

Sending me up here was about the stupidest thing you've ever done. If you think you can make me forget my friends, you're crazy. I heard you telling Mr. Fair-clothe next door that I was out of control. That's dumb. I know exactly what I want. And it's not up here on this mountain. Don't bother coming after me, I won't be here by the time you arrive. I hate you, I hate you!

Your son,
Taylor

Taylor folded the letter, stuffed it into an envelope, and addressed it. He lay on top of the quilt fighting off sleep, trying not to think of DeWayne. But Taylor lost the battle, and as he had every night since the accident, he awoke with a fright.

He walked to the window and saw brilliant stars spilling across the black sky over the tops of the whispering cedars. Outside was quiet except for the swish of the wind through the tree branches and a chorus of crickets and toads and other night creatures. Taylor glanced at the antique clock ticking on the dresser. It was past midnight.

He knew it was useless to try to get back to sleep. But this time it was not just the dread of dreaming of DeWayne, it was also the distant sound of a hound dog yelping that kept him awake. Then he heard a *tap, tap, tap* noise coming from the direction of the river, but much closer. It was probably campers. Maybe he could hitch a ride back to town with them.

Taylor picked up his duffel bag and slipped down the stairs. He dropped the poison-pen letter into the wicker box marked MAIL, then tiptoed outside. The border collie, whose name was Lucy, licked his hand and fell into step at his feet as if she had known him all her life. She kept close to his side, stopping when he stopped, running when he ran.

Taylor followed the dirt road, whose white dust twinkled in the pale light of a rising crescent moon. When he was about a mile from the house, the tapping noise and barking sounded very near. A yellow light bobbed in the woods and low voices drifted on the cool air sweet with the fragrance of cedar.

Taylor hunched low and crept closer. He pushed aside the branches of scrub oak and saw a flashlight in the hand of the short, redheaded woman from the flatbed truck they had passed on the road earlier that day. She shined it for the scrawny man and the tall redheaded teenager as they swung their axes at cedar trees.

The post cutters' spotted bird dog growled, then yelped and charged toward the bushes.

Lucy quivered and her throat rumbled, but Taylor grabbed her collar and ran.

Back in the attic bedroom, as he undressed and crawled into bed, Taylor heard the *tap, tap, tap* again.

"Good," he whispered with a smile. "I don't care if the post cutters chop down every single tree on this mountain."

3

Taylor opened his burning eyes. The raspy crow of a rooster blasted under his window. As if answering a challenge, another rooster crowed somewhere at the foot of the mountain. A few seconds later, the rooster below his window screamed again.

Taylor rolled over on his stomach and stuffed the pillow over his head. But the sound was too piercing. With a groan, he tossed back the bedcover and staggered to the window.

"It's still dark outside. What's wrong with you?" he shouted down at the rooster perched proudly on top of a dilapidated wagon grown up with weeds and vines. The rooster cocked its head to one side, stared at Taylor with tiny black eyes, then stretched its neck and crowed with all its might.

Taylor was looking for something to throw at the rooster when someone rapped on the door.

"Breakfast is almost ready," Aunt Etta's

high-pitched voice shouted. "Hope you like flapjacks."

"What I'd like is a good night's sleep," Taylor muttered. He opened the door and squinted out the hallway light searing into his eyes.

"Don't you look a sight." Aunt Etta chuckled, glancing at his disheveled hair and sleepy eyes. "Didn't you sleep well?"

"Sleep? How do you expect anyone to sleep around here with that stupid rooster crowing all night long?"

"We don't expect people to sleep once Old Dixie starts up. He's our alarm clock. Breakfast will be ready in fifteen minutes. If you miss it, you'll get mighty hungry before lunch."

Taylor rolled his eyes as he closed the door. What was the point in waking up so early when there was nothing to do on this forsaken mountain anyway? At home, during the summers, he usually slept till noon, got up for lunch, then messed around with the guys in the Lynch Mob until late at night. He'd put in an appearance now and then, but with his mother's work schedule, sometimes he wouldn't see her for more than five minutes a day. He couldn't understand why all of a sudden she was so concerned with him when she never even saw him.

Taylor crawled back into bed and fell asleep. Old Dixie must have gotten tired of crowing or else was satisfied that he had made the sun come up another day.

A knocking at the bedroom door made Taylor jump. His heart pounded and his eyes wildly searched the room until he realized where he was.

"Time's a-wasting, son. Get dressed." Uncle Earl's voice boomed from the hallway. "We've got lots of work to do today."

Taylor groaned. "I'm going to call child protective services," he muttered to himself. "It must be against the law to make a kid work against his will."

He took a quick shower and slowly woke up, but his eyes still burned. He slicked back his dark hair, frowning as always when a few unruly curls broke free and tumbled over his forehead. He had forgotten to pack his jar of hair gel, so there was nothing he could do.

Taylor jerked on a pair of baggy cotton pants and an oversized shirt. He stuffed his wallet and comb into his pants pockets and slipped a small switchblade knife into his sock. He didn't expect to run across any trouble up here, but a guy had to always be prepared. That was what Jeremy taught him.

Taylor heaved a sigh at the thought of Jeremy. He hadn't heard from him since the day after DeWayne's accident. Even though Jeremy was in Arizona with his real dad, Taylor had expected to hear from him by now.

When Taylor tried to open the bedroom door, it didn't budge at first, and as he stepped out into the hall he saw why. Lucy had curled up in front of the door. She wagged her tail and pushed her nose into his hand.

"Hello, girl. Did Old Dixie wake you up, too?" Taylor knelt down and scratched her head and stroked her long, silky black-and-white hair. "That was some fun we had last night, wasn't it?"

Lucy stepped closer and shoved her nose into his face and licked his cheek. Taylor laughed. "I like you, too, Lucy," he whispered. He buried his nose into her soft hair. The smell brought back memories of something familiar. He was sure they had a dog, a setter, when he was very young, but apparently it disappeared the same time as the hunting guns. His mother probably thought, *What's the point in having a hunting dog if you don't have a hunting man?*

Taylor slapped the side of his pants. Lucy barked and leaped after him down the stairs.

"Well, looks like Lucy has a new friend," Uncle Earl said as he stepped out of the hall bathroom, pulling his overall suspenders over a long-sleeved checkered shirt.

When Taylor reached the kitchen and breakfast room that took up half the bottom floor, he saw that the cheap kitchenette table was cleared of dirty dishes and freshly washed off. The aroma of pancakes and maple syrup lingered in the air. Aunt Etta was putting a pitcher of orange juice away in the refrigerator. Earl turned to her as if to say something, but her lips were set in a tight line and her back moved as she started scrubbing the countertop with a wet washrag.

"Etta doesn't tolerate tardiness or excuses," Uncle Earl whispered near Taylor's ear. "When she says breakfast is ready, she means it. If you don't show up, you miss it. It's the old schoolteacher in her, you know." He winked and steered Taylor to the living room.

Taylor's gaze swept around the room, dark except for the light pouring in through sliding glass doors that led out onto a screened-in back porch. The fireplace chimney and hearth were made of the same white flagstones as the outside walls of the house. The rough wood mantel looked like it was the original, very plain and unpainted. Above it rested an antique rifle, and framed photographs covered the mantel itself. Taylor recognized a few of the faces—his grandparents, his mother, himself as a child, and his father. Taylor stepped closer and stared at his father's smiling face. The photo was a smaller version of the one that his mother had on her bedroom dresser.

"I don't suppose you remember your father," Uncle Earl said, stepping up behind Taylor. "You were just a little tyke when he died. Five years old, as I recall. You probably didn't know what was going on at his funeral."

Taylor swallowed and shifted his weight. He hated talking about his father's funeral or anything else about his father.

"That was almost eight years ago, Uncle Earl. I don't remember much."

Taylor had only one vivid memory of the day of the funeral: his mother had smashed open the gun case and one by one carried her husband's hunting rifles out to her car. Then she stuffed all the boxes of cartridges and shotgun shells into a paper bag. With Taylor strapped into the passenger seat, she drove to a river bridge and threw the rifles and bullets into the dirty water. Taylor, thinking it was a game, picked up a rock, and his small, chubby arms threw it into the dark water, still bubbling where the guns had disappeared.

"He was a fine young man. A father any boy would be proud of."

Taylor shrugged uncomfortably. "I don't remember him."

"Did your mother ever tell you about the accident that killed him?" Uncle Earl asked gently.

"Just that it was a hunting accident. She hates guns because of that."

Earl nodded. "Well, that's to be expected. I suppose she'll tell you all about it some day when she thinks you're ready." He adjusted his worn white hat over his two-tone bald head. "Well, it's time to get on down to the mill."

Taylor glanced at the toaster and the big box of Post Toasties on the countertop. Then his stomach growled loudly.

"We'll get you something to eat down at the store," Uncle Earl whispered. "Just don't tell Etta."

"I'm not hungry," Taylor lied. "I never eat breakfast anyway." And that was mostly the truth. His mom never cooked breakfast; she was always just getting up for work when he was going out the door for school.

Uncle Earl opened the door to a banged-up yellow pickup that Taylor had seen in the front yard. He thought for sure it wouldn't run, but it started up immediately. The inside smelled like tobacco, and Earl instantly lit up a cigarette and blew the smoke out the window.

"Etta doesn't allow smoking inside the house anymore," he said. "Says if I want to go to an early grave with smoking, it's my business, but she'll not go with me from secondhand smoke." He chuckled and shook his head. "My Etta's a hard one to live with sometimes. But she has a heart of gold."

Yeah, just ask my stomach about her heart of gold, Taylor thought, as hunger pain ripped through him.

Uncle Earl whistled for Lucy and she leaped into the truck bed, her lips pulled back in a doggish grin, her tail wagging furiously. Taylor felt something bump his head and when he turned around he saw two rifles in a rack above the back of the seat. As always when he was near guns, he felt a little nervous twinge in his stomach.

When the truck reached a fork in the road, Uncle Earl spun the steering wheel to the right, the opposite direction from which they had come last night.

"I'm taking the scenic route," he said with a chuckle. "I'm in no hurry to get to work. Just don't tell Etta about us goofing off."

"I wouldn't dream of it," Taylor said as he lowered the window the rest of the way. The pickup rattled and the motor vibrated under his feet as it rolled down the dirt road covered with a layer of crushed limestone rock. Some of the pieces still had tiny bits of quartz crystals in them, making the road glitter in the sunlight. Occasionally a piece of rock thudded against the undercarriage.

Blue jays screamed, redbirds sang, and doves fluttered out of the middle of the road. Two rabbits hopped out of nowhere, froze when they heard the pickup, then darted away just a few seconds before it passed by. A metal bell clanged as a herd of goats followed their leader and blocked the road. Uncle Earl honked, then slowed down and tossed a few biscuits out the window.

I feel like I'm touring Safari Land, Taylor thought, as he watched two deer in a clearing twitch their ears then gracefully dart away.

Lucy barked constantly and excitedly walked from one side of the truck bed to the other.

"Lucy loves the morning when all the animals are out. Looky, yonder goes a squirrel. Ever had fried squirrel meat?"

Taylor shook his head.

"Tastes like chicken. So does fried rabbit. Plenty of them up here on the mountain. Lucy likes to hunt. Helps keep the animals from overpopulating. But hunting's too much walking for my old bones. I like fishing where a man can settle back and relax. You like fishing?"

Taylor shrugged. "Naw, it's too boring."

In fact, in all his thirteen years on earth, Taylor had never once gone fishing. He had tried to catch some crawdads and turtles from the bayou that ran behind the school. But it was too polluted for any fish bigger than minnows. It was Jeremy who claimed fishing was boring, after going on a fishing trip with his dad in Arizona. And Jeremy's word was good enough for Taylor.

"Boring, huh?" Uncle Earl's eyebrow shot up. "Well, maybe you've been fishing at the wrong holes. We'll try to go this evening after supper."

The morning air felt cool and smelled sweet with the fragrance of cedar and tangy weeds and grass. Taylor leaned his head out farther, not unlike Lucy who stuck her nose in the breeze, her eyes shut and her lips parted in a smile.

The pickup rattled down the mountain, not passing another living soul. Only a few houses—mostly small vacation cabins—dotted the top of the mountain. When they arrived at the bottom of the mountain, Taylor saw that the lights were already on in the bait house and the general store.

"Looks like Lecil got an early start this morning. We'll get you some breakfast, but Lordy, Lordy, don't tell Etta I let you have junk food. She'll be all over me."

The pickup squealed to a halt and Lecil looked up from over the cash register. Taylor selected some chocolate cupcakes, a pint of milk, and a granola bar with chocolate chips. That was about as close as he ever came to health food.

Two fishermen stood at the counter, sipping coffee from Styrofoam cups. The coffee pot steamed at the back of the store near a huge old-fashioned metal ice chest full of soft drinks. The men exchanged small talk with Earl about fish and bait and tackle and lures, while Taylor ate the cupcakes. He was only interrupted once, when Earl introduced him as "Ginny's boy" to the fishermen.

Taylor was almost asleep again when Earl got back into the truck and they drove over to the gristmill, about a hundred yards down the road.

"Here she is. Butler's Mill. Your great-great-grandpa Tobias Butler built this back in 1848, with the help of his two brothers. Raised five sons and three daughters. All but one of those boys were killed in the Civil War. The only reason the fifth son lived was because he was too young to go to war. That was your great-grandpa William Bradley Butler."

Taylor shifted his weight and tried to not roll his eyes in boredom. The last thing he wanted to hear about was a bunch of dead relatives. All the time Uncle Earl was talking, Taylor was trying to think up some way to get out of working at the gristmill. Not because he hated work, but because of the principle of it all. The most logical thing for him to do was to hitch a ride with someone and run away. But it looked like every person on the mountain and every fisherman in the county knew Earl, and now, thanks to Earl's constant prattle, they all knew Taylor, too. It would have to be a stranger that he hitched a ride with.

"Looky here, let me show you something." Earl walked around to the back side of the gristmill, near the wooden paddle that slowly turned from water trickling over it. "All five of the Butler boys carved their names in this rock. Samuel, Thomas, Lorenzo, Gabriel, and William."

Earl reached over and yanked up some weeds, then brushed away a blob of dirt. He tilted his sweat-stained hat back and clucked his tongue.

"What a waste of young men's lives. Guess all wars are like that."

Taylor surveyed the smooth tan-and-white flagstones on all sides of the mill. What a great place to tag. If he had a can of spray paint, he could make the place come alive. Nothing as boring and unnoticeable as names carved in stone.

As they walked around to the front entrance, they passed under an old sign. The paint had been recently refurbished. NO WIDOW WILL BE TURNED AWAY FROM BUTLER'S MILL.

"Tobias put that sign up right after the War

between the States. Lot of the women were widows and didn't have the money to pay him for the grinding of their corn or wheat. He made it his policy not to charge any widow."

"Didn't he lose a lot of money?"

"Probably. But some things are more important than money."

"Yeah, like what?"

"Honor, love, an honest day's work, just to name a few." Earl reached over and tousled Taylor's hair.

"Hey, man, cut it out. It took me a long time to get my hair fixed up."

Earl bellowed with laughter. "Your hair won't be a pretty sight by the end of the day. And you know what, the looks of your hair won't matter one iota by then. I guarantee."

Taylor reluctantly followed Earl into the gristmill, not having a clue what he was supposed to do. Earl flipped a switch and pale golden light flooded the room. The smell of corn and wheat and just plain dirt filled Taylor's nostrils.

Earl flipped another switch and an electric motor shuddered to life.

" 'Course, Tobias didn't have electric motors to grind the wheat. He used an overshot paddle wheel like the one outside. Water from the creek came over the top of the wheel, filled the buckets, and made it turn. The buckets emptied back into the creek at the bottom. The main wheel was hooked up to a shaft, which made these smaller ones turn."

Uncle Earl pointed to three other wheels of various sizes. A sturdy rubberlike belt threaded around each wheel and led to two round stones that looked a lot like Stone Age wheels lying on their sides.

"What are those things?" Taylor asked, trying not to show too much interest. He didn't want the old man to get the wrong idea.

"Those are the grinding stones. Most folks call them birthstones. They're almost a hundred and fifty years old. They were carved in France and then shipped to Texas by boat. Tobias hauled them here by oxen." Taylor reached over and touched one of the heavy rough gray stones. They were smooth on the outside and grooved on the inside.

"You mean you're going to grind the corn with just two big rocks? Doesn't that take a long time?"

"Sure it does. That's what makes it good."

"And all the grinding was done with water power? But that little creek outside doesn't look very powerful." Taylor leaned out a window and looked down at the paddle wheel. The water barely trickled over it.

"You're sharp as a tack," Earl said with a wink. "The creek switched course back in 1944, and we ended up with only half as much water as in the old days, so my daddy installed an electric motor. The war was going on and he didn't have much money. I was in France, knee-deep in trench mud."

He pointed to a lumpy-looking gunnysack on the floor. "Take that sack of dried corn over to the hopper and dump it in. There's a knife on the table."

"The hopper?"

"That big metal funnel sitting over the grinding stones."

Taylor looked at the sack. It must have weighed fifty pounds.

"You did say you're going to pay me for this, didn't you?"

Earl rubbed his chin. "Apprentice wages until you learn how to do it right."

"Apprentice? What's to learn?" Taylor heaved the sack to his shoulder and staggered across the room. He plopped it on the table next to the hopper, then jabbed the knife blade into the burlap, sawing it with a loud ripping sound.

He lifted the sack as high as he could and shook it. Bright yellow corn seeds spilled all over the table and floor, and some even went into the hopper. He turned around and glared at Uncle Earl.

"Nothing to it. What do you want me to do next?"

Earl rolled a toothpick around in his mouth a couple of times.

"We usually save the tow sacks and reuse them," he said. "Guess it takes a while to get the knack of it. Let me show you." He hoisted another filled gunnysack on his shoulder like it was a lunch box, plopped it on the rim of the hopper, cut the cord tied at the top, and shook the sack as the contents neatly spilled into the container. They sounded like hail on a tin roof as they traveled down the hopper funnel to the space between the two turning stones. A racket filled the air as the stones began pulverizing the corn.

Slowly at first, then faster, the ground corn spilled over into small cups attached to a conveyor belt. The filled cups marched up the line to an eight-foot-high wood and glass container. It looked and smelled very old. The words NORDYKE AND MARMON CORNMEAL BOLT were painted on the side of it in gold letters. The cups dumped their contents into the top of the bolt. The cornmeal fell like yellow snow from one screen to another, helped by a machine that gently agitated the screens now and then.

Earl saw Taylor watching the cornmeal.

"The cornmeal bolt has three screens of different gauges. The biggest pieces of corn stay on the top screen. The medium pieces fall down to the next screen. The finest stuff, the meal, goes to the bottom. People buy the meal for their cooking, of course. The medium stuff is called grits, and it's used for breakfast cereal. The biggest pieces are used for livestock and chicken feed. Each kind of grain goes to a separate bin. You scoop the meal out with this scooper and put it into sacks of different sizes. You can grind up wheat as well as corn. If you leave the shells on it, it's called whole wheat flour. Now, is all this as clear as mud?" Earl opened up the glass doors to the bins.

Taylor shrugged as he glanced inside. The smell of cornmeal and flour made him go into a fit of sneezes.

Uncle Earl laughed. "Did you ever hear of a flour-sack dress?"

"No."

"Well, in the old days millers put their flour

in sacks made of calico or gingham cloth to attract the female customers. Women saved up the flour sacks and made dresses or blouses from them. It made them use up the flour faster so they could get the next piece of material."

"Sort of like getting a free Batman glass at the hamburger joint," Taylor said with a smile. "Pretty sneaky."

"Yep, Etta was wearing a blue calico flour-sack dress the first time I ever saw her, back in 1940. Pretty as a picture, she was."

Taylor couldn't imagine Aunt Etta being pretty. All she was now was a bag of bones and wrinkles and white hair.

"Go ahead and empty all those sacks into the hopper," Uncle Earl said. "We'll do the corn today and tomorrow, then the wheat on Wednesday and Thursday. We'll save the sugar for Friday. It's so sticky, I always grind it on the last day. Messes up the machine if you don't clean it out real good."

Taylor reluctantly heaved and ripped and shoved bags of corn all morning, occasionally switching places with Uncle Earl who was scooping cornmeal into cloth bags and sewing the tops with an old-fashioned Singer sewing machine.

At lunchtime, Earl closed the door to the gristmill and they walked over to the general store. Taylor grabbed an ice-cold Dr. Pepper from the metal ice chest and gulped down the whole can without stopping. Sweat streamed from his forehead and temples and trickled down his legs onto his socks. His shirt stuck to him as if it had been soaked in water. He could not remember ever sweating so much, not even at the beach when lying in the sun to get a tan.

"Boy worked up a thirst," Lecil said as he spread out some bread, sliced some barbecued beef, and started making sandwiches. Taylor lay down on a rickety cot at the back of the room where a rotating fan hummed.

"He's a hard worker," Earl said. "You'd expect that of Virginia's boy, though."

Those were the last words Taylor heard before falling into a deep sleep. He didn't even eat, although the tantalizing smell of barbecued beef and potato salad made his mouth water.

When he woke up, Lucy was sitting beside him. She smacked her lips and wagged her tail as Taylor sat up. Lecil's beagle lay on the concrete floor and wagged his tail, but didn't bother to get up.

Taylor's body ached from using muscles he hadn't used before, and he could smell his own sweat. He ran his fingers through his hair and felt it fall into his eyes, along with bits of corn-meal and corn grits. Earl had been right about that. At the moment, Taylor didn't care one iota about what his hair looked like.

4

"Well, Sleeping Beauty has awakened from eternal darkness," Lecil said from behind the counter, the cigarette bobbing in his lips. "Come get yourself some lunch."

"Where's Uncle Earl?" Taylor asked as he sat up and rubbed his eyes. From the shadows dancing across the parking lot he knew it was early afternoon.

"Earl returned his nose to the grindstone a couple of hours ago. He said you could help me out here. No need to wear you down to the bone on the first day."

Lecil still wore the stained apron from last night. Or maybe it was a different one, with fresh bloodstains. He carried a barbecue sandwich and a bag of chips out to the picnic table under the cottonwood tree, then set a tall glass of iced tea beside it.

Taylor devoured the food and drank all the tea.

"Did you cook this barbecue?"

Lecil nodded. "Yes, sir. Learned how to cook in the army."

"When were you in the army?"

"Uncle Sam invited me to join his splendid organization in 1968. *It was the best of times, it was the worst of times,* as a man once said." The dragon tattoo moved as Lecil ran a cloth over the table to brush away crumbs.

After eating, Taylor helped Lecil around the store and barbecue café, washing dishes and taking out the trash. After that he worked at the bait house. It wasn't nearly as hard as the work at the gristmill, but it was disgusting to have to handle fishing worms that slid around in the dark brown humus. He thought of all the neat things he could have done with a handful of worms back home. All the girls he could have scared, all the guys he could have grossed out. Jeremy would have come up with something creative to do with the worms. He always had a plan for everything.

Anger flashed through Taylor. He hated this remote mountain. He missed hanging out with his friends and needed to talk to Jeremy. He silently vowed that he would find out Jeremy's address in Arizona somehow.

That evening, back at the stone house, Taylor

ate supper in spite of the fact that he claimed he wasn't hungry. He remembered Aunt Etta's policy and decided he didn't want to take the chance that he would go to bed hungry.

After supper, while Aunt Etta sat in the corner crocheting, Uncle Earl worked on wooden cutout figures in his shop beside the house. Most of them were black-and-white cows. Each cow had metal springs attached and a slot to fix a garden hose to, so that when the water was turned on it looked like her tail was swishing water back and forth. Taylor remembered seeing them in people's yards while waiting at the bus stop in Pandora.

It was still light outside and too early to go to bed. Taylor was thinking about turning on the TV when the telephone rang. It was his mother.

"Just calling to see if you got there okay," she said after he took the receiver from Aunt Etta. She sounded tired. Taylor remembered his letter, but knew that she had not received it yet.

"I hate this place," he said right off. "If this is your idea of a joke, then *har, har,* I'm laughing. Now can I come home?"

"Taylor, I've already explained that you have to stay the summer. It'll be good for you. Aunt

Etta says you worked at the gristmill and bait house all day. That's good. I'm sure Uncle Earl is paying you."

"Hah! Not even minimum wage. It's child slavery."

"Well, every little bit helps. You'll have money for some nice school clothes this year for a change. Won't that be neat?"

"Yeah, Mom, really *neat*. If I live that long. The way they're working me, I'll probably die from exhaustion in a couple of weeks."

He heard his mother sigh heavily. "Taylor, I've got to go. I'm on my coffee break. I'm working two shifts all summer. We need the extra money."

"Money isn't everything." Taylor blurted out the words Uncle Earl had quoted earlier. "But it sure seems like it's more important to you than your own son. Fine, go ahead and desert me so you can make a bundle of money. But I won't be here at the end of the summer when you come to get me. *If* you come to get me." He slammed down the receiver.

He had to get out of there or he would go insane.

"I'm leaving," he shouted over his shoulder, and ran out the kitchen door.

Taylor ran as fast as he could for five

minutes, with Lucy chasing after him. He ran until the white dusty road ended near the edge of the mountain—at a gray cliff overhang that gave a panoramic view of the valley and river and other mountains. He saw the road below winding through cotton fields of neighboring farmers.

Lucy sat beside him as he collapsed onto a boulder and hung his legs over the edge. Tears dampened his eyes, but he refused to let them fall. He buried his face into Lucy's soft hair. She whimpered and scooted closer to him, her dark eyes sad with compassion.

"I've gotta get out of this place," he whispered. "Mom doesn't want me, and these old coots want me to be their slave. When I get paid this Friday, maybe I'll buy a bus ticket somewhere—anywhere away from here."

Taylor scratched Lucy's head and she licked his salty cheeks. Suddenly her ears pricked up and she grew tense. Taylor's gaze followed the direction she was looking. At first he didn't see anything, then something red flashed in the cedar breaks directly below.

Taylor spread out flat on his stomach and leaned over the cliff. It was the redheaded teenager he had seen cutting trees last night. This time the boy was aiming a rifle at something.

The spotted bird dog at his feet was frozen in a pointing stance.

Suddenly the rifle jerked and a second later the crisp sound of a gunshot cracked in the air. The dog yelped and ran into the bushes, coming out in a minute with a limp rabbit.

"He got it," Taylor whispered. "That boy knows how to shoot."

The redhead placed the gray cottontail rabbit into a gunnysack strapped to his shoulder. Then he whistled for the dog and slipped into the woods. His tall, lanky frame gracefully dodged the limbs as he cut through the cedars and shrubs.

His body build was a lot like Jeremy's, but Taylor doubted that this boy was as interesting as Jeremy. Even so, maybe he could catch a ride to the Pandora bus stop with the post-cutter family later in the week.

It was dark by the time Taylor slipped back into the house. He closed the door gently and tiptoed across the living room, but Aunt Etta was in her rocking chair, dressed in a flowered cotton housecoat.

"You can stay up late, but you'll still have to get up at dawn. And don't forget to write your daily letter" was all she said before turning out the light and going into her room.

After taking a quick shower and slipping into his pajamas, Taylor stretched on the bed, staring at the rafters and the bare lightbulb. As usual, he tried to fight off the memory of DeWayne's accident. After thirty minutes, he threw the covers back and grabbed a pen and paper and jotted down a letter.

Dear Packer,

I'm real sorry you got sent to juvenile detention. If you'd only been two years younger, like me, you would have been released to your parents. Man, that's cruel. When do you get out?

In case you didn't hear, Mom sent me away to live with these old relatives on top of a mountain. Talk about being in the sticks! The nearest hick town is at least twenty miles away and doesn't have any good video games. You can only get one station on the TV up here. Man, it's like being in a time warp. They drink water from a well. She makes her own soap. Lye soap. I'm afraid to use it. It might eat the flesh off my bones or something.

This old aunt used to be a schoolteacher and man is she mean. The old uncle just wants to work all the time. And he expects me to work with him. You may be in jail, but at least you're in civilization. I'll probably die from boredom before the summer's over, if a rattlesnake doesn't get me first.

My room's in the attic with only one way out. Guess they don't trust me. Mom must have told them I got in trouble with the law for swiping some junk. They probably think I'm going to slit their throats in the middle of the night. Not a bad idea.

Have you heard anything more about DeWayne? The newspaper said he was in a coma and may not live. Jeremy told us all those paint-remover fumes did to him was make him puke. I know Jeremy wouldn't have hurt DeWayne on purpose, so I guess he's got a stronger head. Maybe if we hadn't run away, the ambulance would have gotten to DeWayne in time. Jeremy says to keep our mouths shut and stick together no matter what, and Jeremy is right most of the time, so I guess we did the best thing. Didn't we?

Hope you write me back. It's lonesome

up here on top of Old Smoky (ha! ha!). Hang in there and remember: *Friends before Family—Northside Lynch Mob Rules Forever!*

Your fellow Lyncher,
Taylor Ryan

P.S. Do you know Jeremy's new address in Arizona?

As he crawled back into bed, and just before he drifted to sleep, Taylor heard the *tap, tap, tap* of the post cutters busy at work.

5

The next morning when Old Dixie stretched his neck and screamed out his challenge, Taylor was ready. He opened the nightstand drawer and took out some small stones he had picked up. Through sleepy eyes he aimed and threw the first rock. It smacked the trailer rail that Dixie perched on.

The rooster squawked in midcrow, flapped his wings for balance, and screeched again.

"Oh yeah?" Taylor muttered and grabbed another stone. He aimed again and this time it cracked against the opposite side of the trailer. Old Dixie hopped down and investigated the rock.

"You're not supposed to eat it, stupid. Here's another little snack for you to chew on." Taylor leaned out the window and sent the rock hissing through the air. It hit at Dixie's feet, making the rooster squawk and leap into the air. Fussing and flapping his wings, he strutted to the fence post a few feet away, stretched his neck, and crowed even louder than before.

"Next time, I'll use something more permanent," Taylor shouted. "And we'll have chicken and dumplings for dinner."

He selected some clothes. No use in trying to go back to sleep. The old bird was making sure of that.

Taylor rubbed his shoulder and upper arms, trying to massage out some of the ache deep in his muscles. Last year Jeremy's folks bought him a weight-lifting set for his birthday and the Mob all took turns. They decided they would be ready for anyone who dared to come into their territory. Taylor's arms and legs had ached back then, too. But that was different. That was something he was doing for fun.

A tap on the door and Aunt Etta announcing that breakfast would be ready in ten minutes sent Taylor scurrying to the bathroom. He slicked back his hair and jerked on a pair of shorts and a thin T-shirt. No use in dirtying up his good clothes. Besides, there were no other kids around to impress. Just a bunch of old folks like Etta and Earl and Lecil.

As Taylor sat down before a stack of pancakes, bacon and eggs, orange juice, and milk, he reminded himself to ask Lecil about that dragon tattoo on his right arm. He looked like the kind of guy who had fought in at least two wars. Lecil wasn't so bad. At least he wasn't but half as old as Uncle Earl.

As the pickup bounced along the dirt road, once again taking the scenic route, Taylor counted the rabbits along the road. Each one reminded him of the redheaded boy yesterday. He wondered how hard it would be to shoot a rifle. But since his father's hunting accident, his mom wouldn't let Taylor so much as play with a toy gun in the Kmart store, much less handle a real one.

"Uncle Earl, is it rabbit hunting season right now?"

Uncle Earl pushed his hat higher up on his head. He scratched behind one ear.

"Ain't no such thing as rabbit season."

"Oh, you mean it's illegal to shoot one any time of the year?"

"Nope, I mean it's rabbit season all year round."

"Anybody can shoot a rabbit anytime?"

"Sure."

"Won't that make them become endangered?"

Uncle Earl chuckled. "You don't know much 'bout rabbits, I take it."

"We had one in Mrs. Tangelo's class. A brown-and-white one with floppy ears."

"Well, cottontails do two things better than any other animal on the mountain. They sneak into your garden and they multiply. When the Good Lord said go forth and multiply, old brother and sister rabbit sure took His advice to heart. Mama rabbit has dozens of younguns every year. Lots of them get eaten by other varmints, but believe me, there're plenty of them left over to cause trouble with the farmers. Why you asking all this? You got a hankering to go rabbit hunting? Elvis is the dog to take with you. Best rabbit hound dog in the county."

"Elvis?"

"That's Lecil's dog. The brown-and-white beagle you saw sleeping under the minnow tank. Gets real cool under there where the water drips. If you want to go hunting, get Lecil to take you. He knows every tree and cave in these mountains. Of course, that's where he hid out while he was on the lam."

Taylor wrinkled up his nose and turned toward Uncle Earl.

"What does that mean, on the lam?"

"It means he was running from the law."

"Lecil? He broke the law?"

"Sure. He doesn't make a secret of it. He served his time, now he's out on a work-release program. Reports to his parole officer every month."

"What was he in prison for?"

"Murder. But he's really a sweet guy. He was really sorry he did it and hasn't hurt a fly since."

Taylor gulped. Now the way Lecil had chopped the barbecue, the cleaver slicing the meat quickly and confidently, took on a new meaning.

Taylor slumped back into the car seat and stared straight ahead until the pickup reached the bottom of the mountain and squealed to a stop in front of the general store. The lights were on and Lecil's shadow moved across the pulled shades as he swung the meat cleaver again and again on the chopping block. Taylor felt a shiver race down his spine. How could he have misjudged someone so badly?

"Wanta come in and get a Dr. Pepper or something for later on this morning?" Uncle Earl asked.

Taylor opened the pickup door. "No, I'm stuffed from breakfast. I think I'll walk on down to the gristmill."

"I was going to say you can work here at the store and bait house all day, if you'd rather. I know the mill work is hard labor."

Taylor slid down from the seat and shook his head.

"No, actually I don't mind the lifting. I need to build up my muscles. I've been looking kind of wimpy lately."

"Sure 'nough? Okay, suit yourself. Here, take the key and unlock the mill. Turn on the lights and go ahead and get the motors warmed up. I'll be down in a minute."

The morning breeze caressed Taylor's face as he walked down the road. Mourning doves flew in all directions as he approached the mill, rattling soft noises in their throats, and sparrow wings cracked as their flock rose in front of him. Blue jays squawked loudly and red cardinals made high-pitched chirps. One large black crow cawed and flew so close, Taylor had to duck.

Taylor had never seen so many birds, but as he stopped to unlock the door, he noticed corn and wheat seeds all over the ground, spilled from the gunnysacks. The gristmill served like a gigantic backyard bird feeder. His mom loved birds. She left bread crumbs on the apartment balcony all the time and had always insisted on visiting the aviaries at the zoo. It seemed like a lifetime ago that he had gone to the zoo with his mom, or anywhere else for that matter.

Taylor's muscles ached and he groaned like the gristmill motor as he began heaving sacks of seeds. By noon, he was ready for the chipped barbecue sandwich and ice-cold tea. Lecil served their food out under the clacking cottonwood tree, and the dry breeze lapped away their perspiration. Taylor tried not to stare at Lecil's tattoo, but he could not tear his eyes away from the twisting green-and-red dragon.

"She's a beauty, isn't she," Lecil finally said, and rolled his sleeve up all the way.

Taylor gulped and almost choked on a pickle slice.

"I—I didn't mean to stare."

Lecil dismissed the apology with a wave of his stubby fingers.

"Most folks can't take their eyes off it. That's why I wear long sleeves most of the time. Some folks are repulsed by tattoos."

"No, no, I think it's—it's *neat*. Where did you get it?"

Lecil took another puff on the cigarette stub in his mouth.

"Saigon, 1969. In a little tattoo shop off Rue des Cochons. Street of Pigs. I was stinking drunk. The man could have taken advantage of me; he could have done a half-baked job, but he was an honorable man. He poured his heart and soul into it. It's alive, you know." He flexed and unflexed his biceps, and the dragon jumped to life.

Taylor had the sudden urge to dive under the table for cover, but he could not take his eyes off the pulsating dragon.

"Lecil, put that thing away. You're going to scare my customers off," Earl complained as an elderly couple got out of a minivan that had stopped in front of the store. Lecil laughed and rolled his sleeve down.

"Who did you say he murdered?" Taylor whispered to Earl.

"His wife. But he was real sorry. He hid up here in the mountains for a month. The police didn't have a clue where he was. He could have easily escaped and gone to Mexico. He speaks Spanish like a native, you know. But he felt guilty and gave himself up without a fight. Said he deserved to serve time. The jury felt sorry for him, being a Vietnam vet and all, and he was having a bad flashback when he killed her. Got sentenced to only thirty years. Served fifteen of them. A model prisoner—never caused any trouble—so they let him out for a work-parole program. I didn't hesitate hiring him. His dad and I were trench buddies in World

War II. I know how a war can make a normal man go crazy. Lecil is the best cook I've ever had. People come from miles around to eat his barbecue. 'Course, the sauce recipe is mine. Got it up here in my secret vault." He tapped his finger against his head. "Nobody knows the ingredients."

"Not even Lecil?"

"Nope. I mix up the sauce myself by the gallon." Earl rose to his feet, cleaned off the table, and dumped the scraps into an empty oil drum that had been painted bright blue and served as a trash barrel.

"I was thinking," Earl said as he stretched and put his hat back on, "we're almost caught up on the mill work. Mr. Slocum won't bring in his grain until tomorrow morning. Whatta you say you and me knock off early and go fishing? We won't tell Etta. Just surprise her with a string of catfish. You like to eat catfish?"

The only fish Taylor ever ate was the kind served at Long John Silver's or Captain D's fast-food restaurants. He wouldn't know a catfish from a dogfish.

He shrugged. "It's okay."

"Okay? Well, you haven't lived until you've eaten Etta's catfish fried up in home-ground cornmeal, served with fresh turnip greens from the garden. Makes my mouth water just thinking about it. Let's hurry up and finish that last batch of corn, then get our tackle."

True to his word, after finishing a few more sacks of corn, Earl locked up the mill. He kept extra fishing poles and tackle at the bait house. They filled a minnow bucket with lively minnows, a paper cup with humus and wiggly worms, loaded Lucy and Elvis in the back of the truck, and drove to the Brazos River.

The graceful bank willows swished in the breeze, and the cottonwood leaves clacked in harmony. Earl backed the pickup onto a rock ledge right down at the water's edge.

"I'm not one for walking more than I have to," he said with a chuckle. He lifted out a couple of lawn chairs, an ice chest filled with beer, and a portable radio. He flipped on soft country-western music and lit up a cigarette.

"Fish love being serenaded. Catfish round here prefer Merle Haggard or George Jones. Just breaks their little hearts and they come right up to the surface weeping."

Taylor gritted his teeth. If the Lynch Mob knew he was sitting on the banks of a river with a fishing pole, listening to country music, they would all die from laughing.

Taylor wrestled with the fishing rod, refusing help. He grimaced as he watched Earl slip his hook through the body of a fat, wiggly worm.

"Pick out one of those red tails if you're fishing for bass. Grab a worm if you're fishing for catfish. Etta can cook up either one good enough to make you cry."

Yeah, and I want to cry right now from boredom, Taylor wanted to say. He hadn't played a video game in three days and felt withdrawal symptoms moving in. His fingers itched to flip levers, to push buttons, to turn joy sticks. His eyes longed to dart from side to side as he coordinated his movements with the screen. His ears longed to hear the shouts of monsters being killed or the grunts of men being kicked and punched or the screams of maidens in distress. Instead all he heard was the whine of some country singer floating over the peaceful river and the lazy drone of grasshoppers and locusts.

Taylor was fighting off sleep when he heard a noise in the water and jumped with a start. Uncle Earl had fallen asleep, the rod handle at his feet firmly planted in the mud.

"Great," Taylor muttered as he reeled in his line and saw that the hook was bare. He put another worm on it and tried to cast out, but the line got caught in the willow tree behind him. Suddenly Lucy's ears perked up and a growl rumbled in her throat.

Taylor heard the splash of a lead sinker hitting water and saw a flash of red hair and denim overalls about twenty yards down the bank. Then he saw the familiar spotted bird dog walking in circles, its nose to the ground.

Lucy yelped, then Elvis darted after the strange dog. Uncle Earl snorted and jumped. "What happened?"

"Lucy and Elvis just took off after that post cutter's dog."

Earl stood, stretched, and reeled in his line.

"Something bit while I was dozing. Didn't you see the line quivering?"

Taylor shrugged. So that was what the quivering line meant, a fish on the end of it. "I wasn't paying attention to your line. I had my own problems."

Earl glanced up at the line tangled in the tree and shook his head.

"Hmm, I see that."

When the dogs began snarling and yelping and snapping at each other, Earl shouted, "Lucy, come here!" The border collie crept back, her head low and her tail between her legs. But Elvis kept sniffing and circling the other dog.

The dogs growled and their hair stood on end until suddenly a sharp, demanding whistle pierced the air. The bird dog reluctantly turned around and returned to the riverbank. The redheaded boy walked to his dog, muttered something under his breath, then approached Uncle Earl. He removed a green-and-yellow John Deere tractor cap from his head.

"Sorry 'bout the dog, Mr. Butler," he said softly. "Spotty loves a good dogfight. Can't hardly keep him away."

Earl nodded. He noticed that the boy held a stringer with three fish on it.

"Fish biting okay?"

"Yep, purty good. I saw that old yeller cat while back."

"How long you been here?"

" 'Bout thirty minutes."

"Leaving already?"

"Have to. Just snagged my last hook on that rock ledge 'bout twenty feet out."

"Yep, that ledge has taken many a fisherman's hook. You're welcome to take some of mine."

Uncle Earl opened his green plastic tackle

box. The upper rows of slots glided up and out of the way to expose the lower compartments. Lures, hooks, string, bobbers and corks, lead weights, a gutting knife, and insect repellent— each item took its place neatly in its assigned slot.

Taylor heard the redhead draw in air sharply.

"That's the prettiest tackle box I ever saw, I swear."

"Thanks. What size hook do you need?"

"I couldn't take your hooks, sir."

Uncle Earl grabbed a small pack that contained about ten hooks and held it out to the boy.

"Go ahead."

The boy ran his long, skinny fingers through his unruly red hair and glanced across the river.

"Pa told me not to take charity from anybody."

"You're Vernon Sinkler's boy, aren't you?"

The boy's brown eyes looked startled. He stepped back, frowning.

"It's okay. I know your pa. This isn't charity, it's just a loan. You can pay me back later. And tell your pa to stop by the rock house or the mill. I've got a stand of blackjack that needs to be thinned out."

The boy took the hooks. "I'm obliged, Mr.

Butler. I'll repay you as soon as I can. And I'll give Pa the message." He put his cap back on, glanced at Taylor, and nodded.

After the boy had gone, Earl rebaited a hook and cast out his line. It hummed as it unreeled, then landed with a soft plop.

"That boy has too much pride. Hasn't learned the difference between charity and just plain being neighborly. Guess that comes from being a Sinkler."

To Taylor's surprise, he caught five fish and Earl caught none. Three were pretty good size catfish. When he reeled in the biggest one, he almost forgot that he wasn't having fun.

That night, true to Earl's promise, Aunt Etta fried up catfish rolled in cornmeal, in spite of the evil eye she cast on him when he came through the door holding the stringer of fish, his feet and pants all muddy.

His stomach full and his body weary, Taylor barely had time to scribble a quick note to the Spencer brothers before falling asleep by ten o'clock.

Dear Eric and Errol,
    You'll never guess where I am. On top of a mountain in the middle of nowhere.

My mom sent me packing to this old aunt and uncle. They are slave drivers. I've done nothing but work like a dog since I got here. Could you send me the number of the child-abuse hotline? I'm going to report these old coots to the authorities.

And do you have Jeremy's address in Arizona? I need to get his advice on something.

I get to feed all the worms and minnows they sell as fish bait. It's really gross. Imagine what a scream we could get out of Brandi with a handful of worms?

If you hear any news about DeWayne, let me know. They don't get any city newspapers up here and I don't dare mention it to my mom or she might get suspicious. I haven't told anyone what happened, have you? Jeremy said not to talk to anyone, but it's hard, isn't it? Wish the gang hadn't broke up. Wish I had never met DeWayne.

I don't plan to stay here much longer. One way or another, I'll get back. Maybe I can stay with you guys and hide in your closet like I did a few times last summer.

Man, I'm dead tired, so I've gotta close this letter.

Northside Lynch Mob Rules Forever!
Your fellow Mob-head,
Taylor Ryan

Taylor didn't even hear the tap of the post cutter's ax and the buzz of the chain saw as he fell asleep. And he only thought of DeWayne in his dreams.

6

The next morning, Taylor woke up five minutes before Old Dixie stretched his neck and crowed at the rising sun. As he opened the bedroom door, he saw a clean pair of overalls and a long-sleeved shirt hanging on the knob. Uncle Earl was tiptoeing down the stairs. He paused and looked up.

"I noticed you had some scratches and scrapes on your arms and legs. Grinding corn can be hazardous sometimes. Not to mention exploring the woods. Thought you might want to wear something more protective than those shorts."

Taylor touched the thick denim, now soft from years of washings. No way he was going to be seen wearing hillbilly clothes like that.

"They look hot," he said, hoping Uncle Earl wouldn't press the issue.

"They're right comfortable, but suit yourself. Our grandson always jumped into them the minute he walked through the door. 'Course, that was many a year ago." He continued down the stairs.

In the bathroom, Taylor looked at the cuts, scratches, and bruises all over his body, especially on his arms and legs. He didn't remember how he got any of them. He considered wearing his good clothes but dismissed it and put on shorts again.

He bounded down the stairs to the kitchen. Aunt Etta was frying eggs and bacon.

"My word, you're up early this morning, Taylor. You must have gotten a good night's sleep."

Taylor shrugged. "Not especially." He dropped the letter in the mail basket, then poured himself a tall glass of orange juice. He sat at the kitchenette table and sipped the juice.

"Aunt Etta, do you know the name of that Sinkler boy? The tall redheaded one?"

Aunt Etta held the spatula in midair a moment and stared into space.

"Well, I know the names of every student I ever taught for forty-five years. Let me see. His mother is named Lavinia and, of course, his father is Vernon. They grew up in these parts. I taught him in eighth grade and taught her while I was substituting for the sixth grade for a week. Seems like the oldest boy was named after Vernon's pa. That would make it Jesse Lee. I'm pretty sure that's it. Jesse Lee Sinkler."

She scooped two eggs from the skillet and slid them onto a large, ceramic plate that looked like it weighed a couple of pounds. She put the bacon in a plate lined with paper towels to absorb the grease and placed it in the middle of the table beside a big bowl of hominy grits and a basket piled high with biscuits.

Uncle Earl came through the back door, scraping his feet on the mat, holding a jar of honey in one hand.

"We're down to our last jar," he announced, as he pulled up a chair and removed his hat. As usual, he looked different with the sharp tan line across his brow. Taylor wondered why Uncle Earl didn't just go without his hat a few times during the summer to get tanned on the bald place, so it wouldn't look so weird.

"Earl, what's that oldest Sinkler boy named?" Aunt Etta asked. "Wasn't it Jesse Lee?"

Earl scratched behind one ear. "Hmm, come to think of it, you may be right. Old man Sinkler was Jesse Lee. Far as I know, those Sinklers have had a Lee in their name back since the Civil War. One of them served under

General Robert E. Lee, got some kind of medal."

"Too bad the family line dwindled down to Vernon."

"Now, Etta. Vernon wasn't always so bad. He was a real hero in Vietnam, remember?"

"Maybe so, but that doesn't make excuses for what he did with his life. Vernon Sinkler threw his talents away."

Earl clamped his mouth shut and poured creamy white gravy over a biscuit on his plate.

"I don't feel like arguing with you this morning, Etta Mae, but you know you're wrong. Just 'cause a man is as poor as Job's turkey doesn't mean he's a failure."

"I never said that. All I said was that Vernon Sinkler wasted his talents. I remember when I taught him eighth-grade language arts. He was sharp as a tack. He could recite every poem in the literature book. All I had to do was read it aloud once and he would know it by heart."

Taylor knew a girl in the seventh grade like that. Always learned fast. He envied her because it always took him a long time to memorize things, especially poetry, which he hated in the first place.

"But Vernon hated to read," Aunt Etta continued as she removed another batch of biscuits from the oven. "He would stumble over the words, stutter, get frustrated, and slam the book on his desk. Wish I had a nickel for every time Vernon Sinkler got mad and threw his book across the room. That was why I had to fail him. He had no respect for authority and no discipline. I knew he had the intelligence to be an A student, but I couldn't reach him. He broke my heart. He was one of those boys who fell between the cracks. I know I could have reached him if he had only stayed in school the rest of the year."

"Mr. Sinkler dropped out of school in the eighth grade?" Taylor asked, looking up over the stack of biscuits. He had never met anyone who dropped out so early. Packer's older brother dropped out in tenth and Packer had flunked twice and was now in juvenile detention, but even he had managed to scrape through the eighth grade. Taylor would be in the eighth grade next year. That meant Vernon Sinkler was just about his age when he dropped out of school.

"He surely did," Aunt Etta replied. "Got furious one day when a bunch of kids laughed at him. It was 'The Charge of the Light Brigade' he was trying to read. I ran after him, even called his house, but he never went home that day. His mother was in the hospital, and his father was a drinker. Poor Vernon ran into the woods and didn't return home for weeks. By then school was out. If only I hadn't pushed him so hard. Nowadays when children have reading disabilities, they are given all kinds of special treatment and the teachers work with them. Back then we didn't know about things like dyslexia. I could have turned his life around if I hadn't been so strict."

She sighed and slumped into the kitchen chair. Uncle Earl reached across the table and cupped his rough, tanned hand over her tiny white one.

"Now, Etta Mae, it wasn't your fault about Vernon. Nobody could have saved that boy. His ma was sick all the time, and his pa was the town drunk. It was only a matter of time till he dropped out of school. It wasn't you that caused it."

Aunt Etta glanced into Earl's blue eyes and forced a weak smile. Her own eyes glistened with water. She stared at Taylor for a minute, then her eyes narrowed.

"Now, I won't hear about *you* dropping out of school, young man. If I have to, I'll come down to that big city and hog-tie you to your desk." She stood, wiped her nose on her apron, then returned to the stove. "Last cup of coffee, Earl."

"No thanks. We're running a little late. There's been a change in plans. Got to clean the equipment and grind the sugar today." He stood, shoved his hat on his bald head, and nodded at Taylor. "Time to hit the road."

By now Taylor was used to the bumps and jolts of the pickup. Even the rocks thumping against the underframe didn't bother him much. He counted the rabbits and squirrels as they rode along in silence. Today Uncle Earl seemed lost in his own thoughts. By the time they reached the bottom of the mountain, Taylor had counted nine rabbits and seven squirrels, though he might have been double counting sometimes because those squirrels had a way of moving around a tree so that you weren't sure if they were coming or going.

It was Wednesday and the motel rooms had to be cleaned for the next batch of fishermen who usually started arriving on Thursdays. Earl gave Taylor the choice of helping to clean the gristmill or the hotel rooms. One glance at the toilets in the rooms and another glance at Lecil's dragon tattoo, and he opted for the gristmill.

It wasn't as bad as he thought it would be.

Just a lot of brushing of loose grist from the equipment with a wire brush. Around nine o'clock a truck rolled to a stop in front of the mill and a very plump man wearing knee-high rubber boots climbed down from the cab. All three of them unloaded heavy bags of what felt like rocks. But when they were opened, it was hard lumps of brown-colored material. Uncle Earl called it raw sugar. It wasn't as hard as rock sugar, but hard enough to keep its form as it was poured into a hopper.

When the ground sugar came out the other end, it was soft and looked just like dark brown sugar, only slightly coarser.

Taylor leaned over and touched it, then jumped back.

"It's moving!" he yelled. "There's something in the sugar!"

Uncle Earl and Mr. Carney laughed, especially Mr. Carney with his small piggy eyes and his round piggy belly. He leaned over, slapping his plump thigh.

"Sure looks alive, but it ain't. It's just so soft and moist that the slightest little movement makes it creep."

"Yep, raw sugar is downright creepy," Uncle Earl agreed. "But it tastes delicious. Your aunt Etta has been baking cookies and pies with it for years. About a hundred times better than the store-bought stuff."

"That's right. Nothing beats the taste of a pinch of raw sugar on top of a bowl of hot cracked wheat on a cold winter's morning."

Taylor picked up a tiny bit in his fingers and placed it on his tongue. It didn't taste like regular brown sugar; it was stronger and more like the flavor of cane syrup, as if you could almost still taste the sugarcane in it.

After a while, Taylor got bored and the smell of raw sugar grew too strong, so he took a break to get some fresh air. He slipped out the back door of the mill and walked down the creek toward the wooden structure that was almost completely hidden in the cedars about one hundred yards from the mill. The white stone chimney served as a guiding beacon as he followed a narrow path. The small round pellets of manure along the way implied that it was now being used as an animal trail, probably Uncle Earl's goats or deer.

In less than five minutes Taylor was standing in front of a genuine log cabin. It had no signs of life except for a bird's nest in the stone chimney located at one end. Pieces of dried mud had fallen out of the grooves between the logs, and some dirt-daubers flew in and out of the chinks.

Morning glories and trumpet vines and an old rosebush rambled here and there over the logs and the sagging roof.

There might have been a front door once, but it was long gone now and some briars had climbed inside through the opening. It was a bright day, but as soon as Taylor stepped inside, his eyes saw only darkness. The musty smell of earthen floors and dirt-daubers' nests and honeysuckle and something very old and very sad all blended into one indescribable fragrance that made his head suddenly go light. He grabbed the door frame, waiting for his eyes to adjust.

Soon he saw the dirt floor, and the stone hearth of the fireplace, still covered with black soot that must have been over a hundred years old. The room was empty except for a big patch of granddaddy longlegs and some pieces of metal equipment that must have been too old for use. Taylor had no idea what they were.

Then he noticed something more recent looking. He saw fresh cornmeal crumbs on the floor and a sprinkling of whole wheat flour.

"Someone has been here," he whispered out loud. Then he saw footprints in the dirt too small to belong to a full-grown adult.

Taylor was turning to leave when he saw

something glistening in the sunlight on the windowsill. He picked up a red hair. It was the exact color of Jesse Lee Sinkler's hair, only it was too long to belong to a boy.

Taylor heard a scraping noise and then a grunt. With visions of wild pigs in his mind, he charged around back. But it wasn't a wild pig, it was a girl with long, red hair scampering down the creek bank on her bottom. She turned around, flashing two brown eyes in a field of brown freckles. In her arms, she held a bag of cornmeal and a bag of flour. Taylor recognized the symbol of Butler's Mill on the side of the bags.

"Hey, thief!" he shouted, and tore after her.

7

Taylor had never seen a girl run so fast, dodging tree branches and leaping over bushes like a deer. He hadn't gone more than fifty feet when a feathery cedar branch smacked him in the face and he fell next to a clump of prickly pear cactus. The girl stopped, turned around, and stared. Taylor must have looked a sight to her, with the cactus needles in his knees and palms of his hands. She may have even felt sorry for him. He decided that his only chance to grab her was to pretend he was hurt and make her come closer.

"Ouch!" He groaned and rubbed his elbow. "I think I broke my arm. Can you help me?"

The girl stood her ground for a minute, then inched closer.

"I'm sorry you got hurt," she said. "It wasn't my fault. You shouldn't oughta chase girls like that." She tossed the mop of red hair back and tried to run her fingers through it, but the bags of meal were too heavy.

"Yeah, I guess you're right, but I really need

help. I can't get up by myself. Just give me a hand and I'll walk away. You won't get into trouble, I promise."

"Trouble? Why should I get into trouble? You were the one chasing me. I'm the girl. You're the nasty ol' boy."

Taylor couldn't believe the nerve of the girl, considering the fact that she was holding two stolen bags of food. He had to bite his lip to keep from giving her a piece of his mind. But Jeremy had taught him that the downfall of all women was feeling sorry for a wounded animal, whether it be a dog or cat or bird or human being.

Taylor faked an attempt at getting up and groaned.

"Geez, girl. Don't just stand there. Can't you see I'm suffering?"

"All I see is a bunch of cactus needles in your behind. That ain't nothing serious."

"All right, suit yourself. Go ahead and leave me here with a broken arm. I don't need the help of a girl anyway. All you'd probably do is mess things up and make me hurt worse than ever. I'd rather depend on a bird dog than a girl your age."

That did it. Her face turned almost as red as her hair. She put the two bags of food in the nook of a cedar tree, then stomped to Taylor. She leaned over.

"Which arm is broken?" she demanded.

"Uh, the right one. Be careful now."

She reached down and grabbed Taylor's left arm and with a grunt pulled him to his feet. Fast as lightning, Taylor grabbed her with his free hand and flung her to the ground and sat on top of her.

"I knew you was fibbing," she shouted, flaying her arms and kicking her feet like a captured rabbit. "Ma told me to never trust men. Now I know why."

Taylor laughed and forced her arms behind her back, then jerked her to her feet.

"Why'd you steal my uncle's cornmeal and flour?"

"We're hungry, that's why. Ma ran out of flour last week, and we ain't had corn bread in two months. Your old uncle won't miss a measly bag of flour and cornmeal. He's got a whole mill full of it. Why, he lets more than this drop to the ground for the birds."

As if demonstrating her words, a flock of mourning doves landed at the cabin and began pecking at the bits of cornmeal that had spilled from her bag. Taylor's heart sank and a wave of guilt washed over him. She was right. Uncle

Earl wouldn't miss a couple of bags of grain.

Taylor was thinking about letting his captive go free when he heard a twig break in the thicket. The girl and Taylor both turned around at the same time and saw the tall, thin redheaded boy standing there, a rifle pointed at Taylor's chest.

"Let my sister go," he said in a calm voice. The dark brown eyes staring down the rifle barrel reminded Taylor of the eyes of an eagle.

"Sure." Taylor released his grip and stepped back. "I—I wasn't going to hurt her. I just caught her stealing my uncle's cornmeal and flour. But if your family is hungry, go ahead and take it. I won't tell anybody."

A look of anguish passed over the boy's face, but he didn't lower the rifle.

"Is that true, Zoe-Linda?"

The girl glanced at Taylor and then at her brother. Taylor could imagine what was going on in her brain. If she said yes, she would get into trouble, but if she said no, her brother might shoot him. Taylor held his breath.

"Yes, Jesse Lee, it's true," she finally muttered softly, and hung her head. Her big toe dug a spot in the ground.

The boy lowered the rifle and set the safety. "My apologies. Zoe-Linda, you know better than that. Mama taught us not to steal. Give back that stuff right now."

"But, Jesse Lee, we ain't had biscuits for a week. I'm hungry all the time."

"I'm fixing to shoot a rabbit for supper, so hush your complaining."

"I'm sick to death of eating rabbit and squirrel every day. I have a hankering for biscuits and thick'nin' gravy."

Taylor thought of the big plate of biscuits that Aunt Etta had made that morning. There was always too much for him and Uncle Earl to eat and the leftovers went to the dogs and the wild birds.

Taylor cleared his throat. "I'm sure Uncle Earl won't mind if you take the cornmeal and flour. Like she said, more than that drops on the ground for the birds."

The girl's eyes lit up and a grin spread across her freckled face.

"See, Jesse Lee, he don't mind."

But the tall boy shook his head.

"Much obliged, but we don't take charity. I'm already owing to Mr. Butler for the fishhooks. I can't take another thing."

"You can pay him back later. He gives credit to everyone around here."

Jesse Lee watched his sister pick up the bags

from the tree nook and cradle them in her arms like twin babies.

"Put them back, Zoe-Linda," he said.

The girl's brown eyes clouded up and began to glisten as she walked to Taylor and gently placed the bags in his arms. He stared at them stupidly as if he were holding real live babies. Jesse Lee took Zoe-Linda's spindly arm, nodded at Taylor, and began walking away. Taylor heard a little sob come from deep in her throat.

"Hey, wait up!" he called out, and trotted up to the tall redhead. "Look, I just thought of something. Would you be willing to trade for the bags?"

A tiny light of hope ignited in Jesse Lee's eyes for a second, then crashed. He ran his fingers through the mop of hair, then shook his head.

"I ain't got nothing to trade for it."

"Sure you do. I've never shot a rifle before. Let me shoot it once for the cornmeal and once for the flour."

Zoe-Linda giggled and grabbed the bags from Taylor's hands, not waiting for an answer from her brother.

"Zoe-Linda, go on home. Tell Ma we didn't take charity."

"I don't wanna go home yet. I want to watch

this here city slicker shoot. Bet he can't hit the broad side of a barn." She grinned in Taylor's face, her dark eyes dancing with mischief.

"Well, if I'm such a bad shot, then maybe it won't be safe for you to tag along," Taylor snapped back. She just giggled some more and fell in step behind Taylor, who was following Jesse Lee through the thicket and the cedars and blackberry brambles along the creek bed. Little scratches and scrapes began showing all over Taylor's arms. Now he understood why Jesse Lee always wore overalls and a long-sleeved shirt even in the summer.

Zoe-Linda tagged along. She slipped once and Taylor felt sorry for her and took one of the bags. After that she held on to his shirttail like a crab.

Twenty minutes later they arrived at a clearing on the other side of the mountain from the log cabin. Jesse Lee picked up an old tin can whose label had long ago been eaten by insects. He placed it on top of a fallen log, then reached into his pocket and pulled out a handful of brass cartridges. He counted them, then slid one into the rifle chamber.

"There's two shells in there now," he said, handing the rifle to Taylor. "This little latch is the safety. Always keep that on until you're ready to shoot. Never point the gun at anyone, even if you think it's empty, unless you aim to shoot him."

Taylor's heart beat faster as he took the rifle into his hands. Without warning the photograph of his father flashed through his head along with the memory of his mother tossing the hunting guns into the river. He swallowed hard and pushed his mother's face from his mind.

The rifle was heavier than Taylor expected and it pulled his arm down. The worn wooden stock felt warm to the touch and the metal barrel felt cold. Jesse showed Taylor how to hold the stock against his shoulder and aim down the barrel through the sight on the end. The smell of gun oil filled his nostrils and brought with it memories of his father cleaning his gun. A memory that he did not know existed until that moment.

"Now, hold your breath while you're shooting," Jesse said. "Old Nellie here pulls to the right, so aim a smidgen to the left of the can to adjust for it."

Taylor nodded. His heart pounded and fear gripped him, even though he knew that there was no way the bullet could turn around in midair and hit him. Still, it was a real gun with real bullets.

Taylor drew in a deep breath and held it as he squeezed the trigger. The recoil thumped his shoulder just as surely as if he'd been shoved by a schoolyard bully. A sharp crack filled the air, tiny pieces of wood leaped from the log, and smoke came out of the barrel all at the same time.

Zoe-Linda snorted, then cackled. "Oh, thank you, thank you, kind sir, for slaying that fierce deadly dragon over yonder." She put her hands over her heart and rolled her eyes. Jesse Lee didn't say anything, but it looked like he was biting back a little smile.

"You did fine," he said. "Most folks couldn't even hit the log on the first try. What happened was, you didn't hold the rifle steady. You let the barrel drop down. This time hold on and keep your eye on the tin can."

Taylor took aim and held his breath again. This time he was expecting the recoil and it didn't scare him. A tiny piece of the log exploded to the left of the can.

Zoe-Linda squealed and clapped. "Whooee, got another one. Yum-yum, we'll be eating delicious roasted cottonwood log tonight." She rubbed her stomach and rolled her eyes. Taylor had a good mind to pick up the bag of flour and dump it on her head.

"Don't pay her no mind. She's half-sappy," Jesse Lee said as he took the rifle and slid another cartridge into the chamber.

"I did what you said, but I still missed." Taylor fought back anger and frustration. "Show me how you do it." He put his hands on his hips and stepped aside.

"I really oughtn't to be wasting bullets on target practice."

"Aw, Pa won't notice one or two measly bullets," Zoe-Linda said. She sat on a big tree stump, rocking back and forth like she had ants in her pants.

Jesse Lee considered for a minute, then lifted the rifle to his shoulder.

"Just one shot." He aimed and squeezed the trigger. The tin can didn't move.

Zoe-Linda got still. Her mouth dropped and her eyes popped wide open. "Jesse Lee Sinkler, I don't believe it. You missed a tin can?"

Jesse didn't say a word but slapped his thigh and whistled. The spotted bird dog came running up behind him. "Fetch," he said. The dog tore into the thicket and came back, a limp rabbit in its mouth. It dropped the dead body at Jesse's feet. Jesse patted the dog and scratched its head.

"Wasn't aiming for the tin can," Jesse said softly.

Zoe-Linda's face went pale and she turned her head away.

"I hate killing things," she said.

"But you don't hate eating, do you?" Jesse said as he stuffed the limp body into a gunnysack tied around his shoulder.

"Well, just once in my life I wish I could eat some store-bought meat. Like hamburger or hot dogs."

"Those things were living animals once, too."

"Maybe so, but I didn't have to look them in the eyes while they was being skinned," she shot back.

Jesse Lee shook his head in resignation. "Women," he muttered, and glanced at Taylor.

"Yeah, women," Taylor agreed. But his stomach wasn't feeling any too good at the sight of the bloody rabbit. And the thought of seeing it being skinned made his own skin crawl. But shooting at tin cans was fun. His friends would be green with envy when they learned he had shot a rifle. Especially Jeremy, who was always bragging about his stepdad's Magnum. The Lynch Mob had tried to break into the gun case more than once, but never could get in.

"Nice meeting you," Jesse Lee said, picking up the bag of flour for his sister. "And much obliged for trading for the flour and cornmeal. Say, what's your name?"

"Taylor Ryan."

"Oh, like old President Zachary Taylor. I love that name," Zoe-Linda said cheerfully. She slipped her arm through Taylor's and looked up, grinning. "Can we play again tomorrow? Let's meet at the log cabin and play a game. Do you have any cards?"

Taylor shrugged. "I don't know. I'm visiting my great-aunt and uncle. I don't know what they've got."

"Well, bring something. I love games. Any games. Even hide-and-seek. I'll bring Vonda Sue and Lawrence along."

"You'll do no such thing," Jesse said. "Leave them at home. Now let's go."

"Wait a minute. Uh, Jesse Lee, I sure would like to target practice with you again tomorrow. Could I trade something else?"

Jesse paused. He reached into his pocket and counted the cartridges again.

"Sorry, Taylor, but I've only got a handful

of shells left. I have to hunt food. Pa would take his belt to my hide if he knew I was wasting bullets on target practice. Sorry."

"What if I bring you some more bullets?"

"Well, I reckon that would be all right. If you use your own ammunition, Pa can't complain."

"Great! What kind do I need to get?"

With his free hand Jesse reached into a tattered leather pouch strung around his waist and pulled out an empty shell box.

"These are my favorite brand."

"What brand is that?" Taylor saw the picture of a red devil on the top, but couldn't make out the writing.

Jesse held the box in front of him and stared blankly at it.

"Jesse Lee can't read," Zoe-Linda piped up.

"Can too," Jesse snapped back.

"Cannot. Prove it. Read them words on the shell box."

Jesse Lee shot an angry glance at her, then cleared his throat.

"Red Devil .22 cartridges," he said slowly. "Best ammo a man can buy." He shoved the box back into the gunnysack. "There wasn't no call for you humiliating me like that, Zoe-Linda." He spun on his heels and tramped into the woods. Zoe-Linda glanced after him, her stubborn chin jutted out.

"Ma says he's as hardheaded as a mule." She turned to Taylor and grinned. "Well, good-bye, my sweet prince. I'll see you tomorrow." She curtsied like a princess and then ran after her brother, hugging the bag of cornmeal to her flat chest.

That night as Taylor lay in bed, he thought about the day's events. One thing he knew for sure: Jesse Lee Sinkler could not read. The picture on the box was a red devil, all right, but the words said "Red Demon."

Taylor imagined shooting at tin cans and what it would be like to become a famous sharpshooter like Annie Oakley. His mom would blow a gasket if she knew he was touching a gun.

As Taylor drifted off to sleep, a new thought worked its way into his subconscious. His mom hated guns; he was now learning to shoot a gun. That was the one thing he could do to get even with her for sending him to this forsaken mountaintop. *As soon as she finds out I'm shooting a gun,* Taylor thought, *she'll bring me back home so fast it'll make your head spin. And then I'll be back with my old gang.*

Taylor got up and took out the yellow notepad with the intention of writing his mother, but he changed his mind and wrote Jeremy instead.

Dear Jeremy,

I don't know your dad's address in Arizona, so I'm sending this to your mom. Hope you get it. I'm stuck up here on top of a mountain, so far away from town it would make you sick at your stomach. Sometimes I think it would have been better to go to juvenile detention with Packer than be up here with these two old coots I'm stuck with.

I went fishing for the first time yesterday. Caught a two-pound catfish. You were right—fishing is boring. Man, I'm tired. The old coots make me work all day like a slave, so that I'm too tired to do anything at night. I wish I were with you at your dad's. I bet you're in the swimming pool right now.

Guess what? I'm learning to shoot a rifle. This guy I met, Jesse Lee, is really an expert shot. When I get back and you get back, maybe we can sneak your dad's hunting rifles out of the case and do some target practicing.

I guess you haven't heard anything about DeWayne lately, since you're in Arizona now. I haven't heard anything else, either, except that he's still in a coma. I hope he comes out of it okay, but it wasn't our fault, was it? How could we know he was going to react that way? If he hadn't been so goofy acting all the time, maybe none of this would have happened. It was his own fault, right? Anyway, don't worry about any of the gang talking. Our lips are sealed—Friends before Family.

Hope you write me soon. I'm going crazy up here.

Northside Lynch Mob Rules Forever!

Your friend,
Taylor Ryan

8

The next two days went by fast for Taylor. His muscles had gotten used to the work and his stomach had gotten used to the feeding schedule. He had even finally broken down and put on the pair of overalls that had belonged to the old couple's grandson. Taylor hated to admit it, but they were comfortable and easy to work in and sure did prevent the grain and weeds and cactus and brambles from scratching him.

Of course, Zoe-Linda made her normal comments about him looking like a field hand. She and Jesse Lee returned to the cabin after supper both days. Taylor was sure that Uncle Earl kept bullets around the house, but he had searched every nook and cranny and all he found were three .22 bullets in the glove compartment of the yellow pickup.

Friday after lunch, Earl closed the mill early. Taylor helped the old couple pick baskets of ripe corn, watermelons, cucumbers, tomatoes, cantaloupes, okra, black-eyed peas, green beans, and yellow squash from a large garden behind the bait house. He heard Aunt Etta banging around in the kitchen for what seemed to be most of the night.

Saturday morning Taylor thought he would get to sleep late. Uncle Earl had already told him that the mill was closed on Saturdays. So when Old Dixie rattled the windows, Taylor rolled over and pulled the pillow over his head and tried to get back to his dream. He wasn't very happy when Aunt Etta knocked on the door as usual before the sun was even up.

"Breakfast in fifteen minutes," she hollered through the door.

Taylor sat up, scratching his head and rubbing his eyes. Still in his pajamas, he walked out into the hall and glared at Aunt Etta.

"Uncle Earl said the mill is closed on Saturdays. Why can't I sleep late?"

"The mill *is* closed today. That's so we can go to town. There's the farmers' market, and grocery shopping, and the hardware store. And Earl needs to buy a new piece of galvanized water pipe. Most country kids can't wait for Saturday to come around. You might even want to spend some of your hard-earned money on a movie at the Palace Theater." She winked.

After Taylor dressed and sat at the breakfast

table, Uncle Earl came in wearing a cleaner than usual pair of overalls. The fringe of gray hair was slicked down with something that smelled like roses. He pulled up a chair across the table from Taylor, then reached into his pocket and counted out ten crumpled five-dollar bills.

"Here's your wages, Taylor. It isn't much, but you're still wet behind the ears. Consider this apprentice wages until you catch on. I imagine that next week your salary will go up ten dollars." He poured thick black molasses syrup over pancakes covered with melted butter.

While the men ate, Aunt Etta scurried around the kitchen loading up jars of jam and jelly. Some were dark purple, others were varying shades of red. Five peach cobblers lined the countertop and the smell permeated the whole house.

"What're all the pies for?"

"Etta sells her cobblers and preserved goods at the farmers' market every Saturday. No sense letting the berries and mustang grapes and wild plums along the fence go to waste. We can't eat all of them."

Taylor helped load up pies, jams and jellies, crocheted afghans, bushel baskets of vegetables, and Earl's wooden cows into the truck bed. Then he squeezed into the front seat. Good thing for him that Aunt Etta was a skinny old broad. The truck bounced along the road more roughly than the Buick ever dreamed of doing, and Taylor's head bobbed back and forth. Lucy rode in the back, yelping at every living thing along the way.

It seemed to Taylor that the truck wasn't going much faster than twenty miles an hour and the dusty road curved endlessly. At last they hit the paved farm-to-market road and picked up speed. The little town of Pandora, that had been so empty and deserted that Monday when Taylor arrived by Greyhound bus, now bustled with activity.

It was pickup heaven at a large open-ended building covered with a high metal roof and located at the edge of town. Rows of stalls had been set up and each one brimmed over with fresh fruits and vegetables or homemade items and foods. Everybody and his dog knew Aunt Etta and Uncle Earl. They raved over Earl's corn, but Taylor thought it looked just like every other farmer's corn.

Etta already had a customer waiting at her booth, wanting a cobbler. Other farmers drove up and unloaded, their hound dogs or bird dogs yelping and sniffing and chasing around. One fat lady set out plates of brownies and cupcakes and a chocolate pie that made Taylor's mouth water, even though he was still stuffed with pancakes. The smell of chocolate mingled with the fragrance of freshly picked vegetables and fruits. Every farmer had watermelons—some long, some round, some green with white stripes, some white with green stripes, some dark green, some pale yellow-green. Every kind had a different name and every farmer knew the kind and sweetness and color by the skin. The booth across from Earl's brimmed with peaches and the sweet smell almost drowned out all other aromas around it.

Taylor helped Uncle Earl unload a wheelbarrow full of yellow-meated watermelons and set up his wooden cows. Etta didn't need any help, as usual, hustling around at breakneck speed. Taylor decided to stroll around. It was early yet. The market didn't open to the public until 10:00 A.M. Some of the booths specialized in homemade crafts, like little windmills for the front yard or dolls in calico cloth that covered your toasters or hand-stitched quilts. Some of the booths had antiques and collectibles, mostly dishes of pink or green or amber-colored Depression glass.

Taylor saw Aunt Etta eyeballing a pink butter platter in the booth across from her. It matched the pink dishes she kept in a homemade hutch in the living room.

After visiting all the booths, Taylor took Lucy for a walk down the street. He knew he wouldn't get lost, the town was so small. He wandered about, to no place in particular. The movie house, the oldest one in the county according to a plaque on its wall, was showing a Clint Eastwood movie and a Stephen King horror movie. Taylor had already seen both of them months ago.

As Taylor walked back toward the farmers' market, he saw a Greyhound bus parked in front of the gas station next to Boyd's Café. He slipped his hand into his pocket to feel the crumpled five-dollar bills. It would be easy to buy a ticket and get away right now—to be free of the gristmill and the goats and the two old coots and the crowing roosters. He began walking toward the bus stop, slow at first, then faster. Suddenly he stopped.

To his right was the hardware store. A large yellow sign with red letters took up most of the front display window. It read: AMMUNITION SALE. Peering through the window, Taylor saw deer antlers, fishing supplies, and rifles hanging on the back wall. He stood in front of the store, his fingers playing with the money in his pocket. He glanced at the rifles, then at the bus. The bus driver was walking out of Boyd's Café, carrying a hamburger and soft drink toward the Greyhound. It was now or never.

"Oh, what the heck," Taylor said as he grabbed the door handle and stepped inside the hardware store. "I'll catch the bus next time I'm in town."

He looked at the boxes of .22 shells under the glass case until he saw Jesse's favorite Red Demon brand. But when he tried to buy them, the owner said he couldn't sell to minors.

"It's only for target practice," Taylor explained.

"Doesn't matter. You'll have to send your daddy in."

"I don't have a daddy. He's dead."

The man frowned and switched his smelly cigar to the other side of his mouth. "Sorry. Then whoever is teaching you to shoot will have to come in. When I was your age, nobody cared a lick if a boy wanted to buy shotgun shells or .22 cartridges. We all knew he was just shooting quail or rabbits or target practicing. But nowadays the government always has to poke its nose into other people's business. They figure now if a boy comes in and asks for shotgun shells, he's just as likely to be fixing to shoot his granny. Or else he might blow his foot off. So the government passes a law that stops all boys from buying shells, even the honest, hardworking ones that wouldn't hurt a fly."

A customer snorted and laughed. Taylor's face turned red and he stomped to the other side of the store. Out of the corner of his eye he watched the counter and when the owner's back was turned to help the customer, Taylor grabbed a handful of cartridges from an opened box on the counter.

He strolled outside as cool as a cucumber, waving to the bus driver as the big silver Greyhound pulled out onto the highway. When he counted the shells, all he had was eight. It wasn't much, but it was better than nothing.

He noticed the Sinklers' old flatbed truck parked across the street in front of Wayne's Feed Store. The little trailer house was not attached this time. Jesse Lee and his pa were unloading cedar posts from the back of the truck. Jesse nodded at Taylor but did not speak. Taylor imagined Jesse would get in trouble with his pa if he stopped, so he kept on walking.

A few minutes later, not far from the farmers' market, Taylor saw Zoe-Linda and a younger boy and girl who looked like twins. All three of them pressed their noses against a glass display window. They spoke to each other in awe-filled voices.

"Isn't that the beautifullest doll you ever saw in your whole life?" the little girl asked, her large blue eyes fixed on a Barbie doll with long blond hair and a frilly pink dress.

"Naw, that's sissy stuff, Vonda Sue," the boy said. "What I like is that baseball glove. Boy, I could have a real game of baseball with that." He pounded his small fist with an imaginary ball.

Zoe-Linda didn't seem to hear her siblings. Her brown eyes stared at a stack of children's books. They were the cheap kind you see in grocery stores, not the big fancy ones you find in real bookstores. The pictures were kind of cartoonish and from their price stickers it looked as if the books had been marked down a few times.

Taylor dodged out of sight into the brick door well of a nearby abandoned building. He figured if the redheaded girl saw him, she would follow him the rest of the day. But after the three children had left, he stepped inside and bought a few of the books. *What the heck,* he thought. They were only fifty cents each.

Each one was a familiar children's fairy tale. He wasn't sure what he was going to do with them, but he figured they would come in handy when dealing with Zoe-Linda.

Those little books came in handy a lot quicker than Taylor had imagined. That evening, after Aunt Etta had sold out of her pies and canned goods, and after Uncle Earl had sold his corn and watermelons and black-eyed peas and two of the wooden cows, they loaded up the dog and came back to the mountain. Taylor was tired from a long, boring day. He had watched the horror movie out of pure boredom and fallen asleep halfway through it. There was nothing that interested him in the clothing stores, so he had most of the fifty dollars still in his pocket.

After supper Taylor walked down the mountain to the log cabin where Jesse Lee had been meeting him the past three days. The redhead was sitting on a tree stump, whittling a piece of wood with a knife. He jumped when Taylor's foot cracked a twig.

"Did you get the .22 shells?" Jesse asked, without so much as a hello.

"Not many. The clerk wouldn't sell to a minor. But I snitched a few off the counter while he wasn't looking. He won't miss them."

"That's stealing."

"Naw, it's snitching. Stealing means grabbing a car from a parking lot. Or a TV or a VCR. This is nothing."

"It's still stealing. I won't be part of it. I'll let you use a couple of my bullets."

Taylor heaved a sigh and wanted to say forget it, but just the sight of the rifle made his fingers itch to fire it again.

"Okay, fine. We'll shoot your bullets," Taylor said, sticking the cartridges back in his pocket.

"All right. By the by, would you give this to Mr. Butler?" Jesse reached into his leather pouch and removed a pack of gold-colored fishing hooks. "Thank him kindly for me."

"Where'd you get the money?"

"Pa sold some cedar posts to the lumber company. He was in a generous mood and gave me five dollars for my week's wages."

Taylor looked at the price sticker on the package of hooks—$2.99. He started to scream child slavery, but the sight of the rifle beckoned him.

This time target practice was even more

wonderful than the first time. He actually hit the tin can on his last try. After three shots, he begged Jesse to use the stolen .22 cartridges, but the redhead stubbornly refused.

"We'll have to figure out another way," he said. "Maybe you could buy some from Mr. Butler."

"I'm sure he's got lots of .22 shells stashed away. I'm still trying to find where he hides them."

"Why don't you just ask him?"

Taylor ran his hand through his hair. "You don't understand. My mom hates guns, ever since my dad was killed in a hunting accident. She would scream bloody murder if she found out I was target practicing. If I find Uncle Earl's bullets, I'll bring a box."

"You mean you're gonna try to steal them, don't you? From your own uncle? I don't want no part of stealing, I told you."

"Okay, okay. I'll *borrow* them. Will that make you happy?"

"Nope. But at least it won't make me feel like a thief," he said as he slung the rifle over a shoulder and turned around to leave.

"One minute, Jesse. I've got something for Zoe-Linda. She's a pain in the caboose, I know, but . . . well, here." Taylor held out one of the picture books. It turned out to be the story of the three little pigs.

Jesse touched the cover and turned each page gently, staring at the words and pictures. He sighed.

"I guess you figured out by now I can't read."

"Don't you go to school?"

"I used to. But we move around so much, I was hardly ever in one place more than a couple of months. And sometimes, if Pa needed me, I'd skip. Pa don't care much about school. He dropped out when he was thirteen. Ma can't read much, either. She wanted me to learn, but Pa has the last word in our house. The teachers said I was a slow learner when it came to reading. By the time I was big, I was too embarrassed to let the other kids know about it."

He closed the book cover. "What is this story about? Why're these pigs dressed up in clothes?"

"This? Aw, it's a kid's book. It's a fairy tale. You wouldn't want to read this."

"Read it to me, Taylor. I just want to hear someone reading the words while I look at them."

Taylor cleared his throat and began. "Once upon a time there were three little pigs . . ."

Jesse's eyes lit up as his friend read the words. Taylor wasn't the best reader in the world, but Jesse thought he was great. Sometimes Taylor missed words or just made words up, but Jesse didn't know. By the time Taylor was finished, Jesse was laughing and slapping his knee.

"That's the funniest story I ever heard." He took the book from Jesse's hands. "Thank you, Taylor. Zoe-Linda will love this."

"Does she read?"

"A little. More than me, but not as good as you. What's this word right here?"

"That is *pig.*"

"Pig. I'll be dogged. Pig. I never dreamt it would look like that. What is this word?"

"That's *wolf.* Look, Jesse Lee, I have to get back before dark, but I've got an idea. Why don't I teach you to read?"

"Naw, I couldn't do that."

"Why not? There's no shame in it. Look, I don't know how to shoot, do I? You're teaching me to shoot, so why don't I teach you to read? We'll make a fair trade. Let's meet here after supper every day."

Taylor held out his hand and, after hesitating, Jesse Lee shook it.

"All right, Taylor Ryan, it's a deal."

That night, after the old couple was asleep, and while the wind whispered through the cedar trees like a dying man, Taylor whipped out a piece of paper and wrote his mother another letter.

Dear Mom,

    I'm beginning to like it here after all. I met a guy who is teaching me to shoot a gun. I tried to buy some bullets, but couldn't, so I stole some. It's getting pretty interesting. Please don't make me come home yet. At least not until I'm an expert shot.

Your son,
Taylor

Taylor stamped the envelope and dropped it in the wicker mailbox. If that didn't make his mother come running after him, nothing would.

9

Sunday morning was about as much fun as getting a tooth pulled. Aunt Etta roused Taylor out of bed and made him dress in his best pants and shirt. He had not packed any ties, so she loaned him one of Uncle Earl's and said, "It won't be noticed on a galloping horse," when he complained that it didn't look cool. Uncle Earl grumbled because he couldn't find his good suspenders and because he nicked his chin shaving. Everyone was in about the worst mood possible as the Buick rumbled down the dirt road to Pandora. The town only had a population of about one thousand yet there were at least six huge churches.

The Buick stopped in front of a white clapboard church with a tall, skinny steeple. A huge live oak tree that Uncle Earl claimed was at least two hundred years old spread its dark green branches over the entire front of the church. A couple of squirrels playing chase in the topmost branches dropped green acorns onto the people below.

Aunt Etta, Uncle Earl, and Taylor walked through heavy wooden doors stained deep mahogany. The smell of floor polish mingled with the scent of women's perfume and Aunt Etta's dusting powder. Taylor wanted to sit on the back pew for a fast escape, but Aunt Etta marched right down the aisle and parked on the third row. Uncle Earl tugged at his tie and shifted his weight constantly while the preacher shouted and pounded on the pulpit. Taylor could swear the man's spit landed on his shoes a couple of times. He supposed the preacher was saying something important, but he also noticed that it was a good way to wake up those men dozing off here and there. Taylor was relieved when the congregation got up to sing the invitational hymn, "Almost Persuaded." The preacher stopped it two times, trying to make it a little hotter for the sinners, making hand gestures as if he were pulling a cow out of mud.

Taylor had never even met the man, but the purple-faced preacher looked right at him when he said, "I know some of you have heavy hearts. You think that what you have done is so terrible that surely God will loathe you. But Jee-sus wants to share your burden. Jee-sus wants to lift that stone from your heart. But only *you* can let him do it. Not your mother; not your father; not your best friend."

Taylor remembered the way DeWayne had looked the last time he saw him, and then he imagined the way DeWayne would look in the hospital, all pale and still with tubes running from his nose and arms. He didn't see how anyone, not even Jesus, could forgive the person who had caused that suffering. Taylor swallowed hard and blocked out the preacher's pleas and concentrated on singing the words to the song. He gripped the back of the wooden pew in front of him until his knuckles turned white. He glanced around and noticed that Uncle Earl and a couple of other people were doing the same thing.

By the time the song was over, three people had walked down the aisle: two to confess their sins, and one little girl to get baptized.

Soon the lights went out and the curtains on the baptismal behind the pulpit went up, revealing an illuminated wall mural of cool blues and greens depicting the River Jordan. The mural seemed to swallow up the minister and the tiny girl, who had changed into white robes. The preacher said a prayer and quoted from the Bible, then dunked her under the water. As they came up, with a loud gurgle and splash, the congregation burst into singing "O, Happy Day." Uncle Earl's deep bass vibrated the pew, and Taylor sang at the top of his lungs, for truly it was a happy day now that the services were over at last.

Afterward, the crowd burst through the heavy wooden front door and spilled out onto the green lawn. Taylor managed to slip by the minister who stood like a guard dog at the front, shaking hands with everyone who passed by.

Kids played everywhere, chasing each other or swinging from the old live oak tree. The women gossiped in little groups and picked up little paper bags of products from the Avon lady. A few of the men, including Uncle Earl, snuck to a patch of evergreens in the far corner and lit up cigarettes. They puffed rapidly, trying to hide the smoke and glancing over their shoulders like punks in the boy's rest room at school.

Taylor didn't know anyone, so he strolled over to the Buick and leaned on the fender. He was surprised when he heard someone shouting his name. He turned around and saw a flash of yellow and red flying across the green grass, heading right for the parking lot.

"Taylor Ryan!" Zoe-Linda cried out, waving a white-gloved hand.

Her yellow dress, a couple of sizes too big, almost dragged the ground. The ruffles and bows swallowed her skinny body. She had washed and curled her mop of red hair since the last time Taylor had seen her. How a brush or comb could ever get through that unruly, thick mess was beyond his imagination.

"Taylor Ryan, you are the most wonderful boy on earth," she said between gasps for breath, then threw her freckled arms around his neck and planted a slurpy kiss on his cheek.

"Whoa!" he said, prying the spindly arms off. "What's going on?"

"Thank you, thank you, thank you for that pretty picture book. I can't believe I've got my very own book now. And Jesse Lee says you're going to teach him how to read. I want to learn, too. Can I?"

"Shh, not so loud." Taylor glanced around. He didn't know anyone, but he had a feeling that associating with the post cutters was not the most popular thing to do.

"Okay, okay. Come with Jesse to the log cabin after supper every day and I'll do what I can. But . . . keep your hands off of me."

She giggled and grinned. "All right. It'll be

our special secret. I love secrets." Her brown eyes sparkled. "How do you like my new dress?" She held her arms out and turned around.

Taylor scratched his head. It was too big and people with her color of hair should never wear that shade of yellow, but what could he say?

"It's pretty," he lied. "What's the special occasion?"

"My birthday, silly. I thought you knew. Wasn't that why you gave me the picture book?"

Taylor shrugged. "Oh yeah, I forgot."

"Mama bought this dress at a garage sale for a dollar. I didn't think I was going to get anything this year, but Mama has a way of stretching a dollar bill. That's my mama over there under the oak tree. And that's the twins, Vonda Sue and Lawrence."

The woman was surprisingly nice-looking. Unlike Zoe-Linda's, Mrs. Sinkler's hair was tied back in a neat style, and the green dress fit her petite body perfectly. The two children were also dressed neatly.

"Didn't Jesse come?" Taylor asked.

"Jesse Lee? No way. Pa makes him stay home and help with chores. Pa says church is for women and sissies. Soon as a boy reaches

twelve, Pa don't want him to go to church anymore. Pa says it makes a man's mind weak.
Poor little Lawrence, it will break his heart. He
loves singing gospel songs more than any child
I've ever seen. He practically has the whole
hymnbook memorized."

Taylor saw Uncle Earl break away from the
smokers and walk toward the Buick.

"Well, we're getting ready to leave," Taylor
said, stepping away from the girl. "I'll see you
and Jesse tomorrow after supper."

"Okay, until then, my darling prince," she
said, and blew him a kiss.

"Whoee," Uncle Earl said with a chuckle.
"My darling prince. You work fast, don't you?
Already got the ladies blowing you kisses." The
old man tried to tousle Taylor's hair, but he
dodged the weathered brown hand.

"I don't know her," Taylor grumbled, but
Uncle Earl teased him all the way to the Rusty
Corral Restaurant down the street from the
church. Apparently Sunday was Aunt Etta's
day off from cooking. While they ate, Taylor
watched the Sinkler flatbed pull up at the
church and the family load onto the back. Zoe-
Linda sat on top of some old blankets to keep
her new dress from getting soiled. As the truck
drove by Taylor saw her hunkered over the pic-

ture book, flipping the pages, and the two other children listening intently. *Well, what the heck,* Taylor thought. *Maybe I'll just teach all of them to read.* He guessed that teaching four wouldn't be much different than teaching one.

That afternoon, Taylor asked Aunt Etta if she had any old schoolbooks lying around. She took him to the attic closet across the hall from his bedroom. The smell of fifty years of dust and moldy books and chalk assaulted his nostrils.

There were books of poetry and grammar and literature. Most of them were too advanced for a beginning reader, but he found some old elementary schoolbooks, tattered and worm-eaten and falling apart. One was about a boy and girl named Dick and Jane.

"This is perfect," Taylor told himself, and pulled them out of the stack.

Later that afternoon, Uncle Earl and Taylor drove down to the river and put out fishing lines.

"Something about sitting through a morning of church zaps the energy from a man's body," Uncle Earl said as they settled in to watch their lines. Before long both of them were sound asleep.

The yelping of Lucy and Elvis woke them

up. Taylor opened his eyes and saw a bearded man, skinny as a rail, standing over the minnow bucket.

"Good afternoon, Vernon," Uncle Earl said.

"Afternoon, Earl. Catching anything?"

"Naw, just a few little perch. We threw them back."

"I heard you was needing some trees thinned out down by the creek."

"Sure, sure. Get in the truck and I'll show you."

The three climbed in the truck, and Earl drove down the dirt road until it turned to no more than two tire tracks in the grass. At last it stopped at a creek at the bottom of the mountain. Before they got out, Taylor could hear the rush of falling water.

"Always said this was the prettiest spot in the county," Vernon said as his brown eyes stared at the clear water spilling over a gray stone ledge and tumbling into a pool about six feet below. The water was so clear, Taylor saw fish swimming. He had the urge to undress and dive in.

"Yep, that it is," Earl said. "Not much a farmer can do with land like this, but it's nice to look at. I need a few of the scrub oak and ashes cleared out. But don't get any of the red-bud trees. Etta would throw a fit if one of her precious redbuds got chopped down."

"Yessir." Mr. Sinkler removed his hat.

"I'll pay you fifty dollars for clearing out the underbrush and thinning some trees. I'll put a spot of yellow paint on the ones I want cut."

"Mighty obliged."

Uncle Earl nodded, then lit up a cigarette. He offered one to Mr. Sinkler, who took it like a starving man takes a slice of bread.

"You finding work all right?" Uncle Earl asked.

Vernon inhaled a deep puff of smoke, then blew it out through his nostrils before replying.

"We're getting by. Mr. Gideon had some post oak and some cedars needed thinning out. Last month was pretty good over in Burleson County."

"You range all the way over there?"

Vernon nodded. "A man's gotta go where the work is."

"You know, I heard they were hiring at Gann's Cotton Gin. You'd make a lot more money at a steady job."

Vernon's eyes flashed and his lips drew taut. "I get by just fine the way I am. I never was one to be tied down to an hourly job. Can't breathe if I have to punch a clock."

"I know exactly what you mean, Vernon. But sometimes a man has to take a job he hates for the sake of his family."

"Are you saying I ain't taking care of my own?" His body stiffened and he clenched his fists.

"Nope, 'course not. Just trying to be neighborly and let you know about the job at the cotton gin. Don't get all riled up. You still going to do this job for me?" Earl waved his hand toward the creek.

Vernon looked at the unfinished cigarette, then dropped it and ground it into the dirt with his boot heel. He glared at Earl a minute, then shoved his hat brim low on his head.

"I'll still do it. After all, a man has to take care of his family." He stomped off, shouting over his shoulder. "I'll find my own way back."

Uncle Earl expelled air from between clenched teeth.

"He's a stubborn mule. Always was and always will be."

"Why doesn't he want to work at the cotton gin?" Taylor asked.

"He's got it in his mind that Mr. Gann wants

to make a fool out of him. They've had a running feud since grammar school. But it's not just Gann, it's all his old classmates. He still holds a grudge against all of them from back when he was in eighth grade and quit. He blames everybody but himself for that."

"That's a long time ago."

"Yep, he's a stubborn man. I guess all he has left is pride. But too much of it."

Uncle Earl didn't talk about Vernon Sinkler any more that day. They returned to the river and fished a little while longer, catching nothing but little perch and watching turtles steal their bait. Taylor wondered what his great-uncle would think if he knew Taylor was going to teach a whole bunch of Sinklers to read and maybe write, too. Taylor didn't think he'd mind, but he sure wasn't going to take any chances and tell anyone, especially Vernon Sinkler. It seemed to Taylor that Vernon was about the most unpopular man in the whole state and the last thing he wanted to do was face off with him. He knew that it would not be easy slipping out and teaching Jesse Lee and his sisters and brother. As far as he was concerned, learning to shoot a gun was a lot more useful than learning to read and write, especially when he returned to the city and took his place in the Northside Lynch Mob. More than ever, he wanted to go back home and get the gang back together.

Taylor could hardly wait till nighttime so he could write a letter to the Spencer brothers. He had to find out what was happening back home.

Dear Eric & Errol,

Tell everyone that I'll be coming home very soon. If I know my mom, she'll freak out when she learns I'm using a gun. Yeah, that's right, a gun. I met this guy, Jesse Lee, and he's teaching me to shoot a rifle. You should see this guy shoot. Never misses. I saw him pick off a rabbit at fifty yards.

Any word on DeWayne? I still don't understand why Jeremy wanted to let him join the Mob, do you? DeWayne was not one of us, he was too sweet or innocent or something. I wish it had never happened, don't you?

Gotta go. These people have me trained to go to sleep the same time as the chickens. That's so I can wake up with this rooster named Old Dixie. Guess you know the first living thing I'm gonna kill when

I learn to shoot. Pow! Chicken and dumplings. Write me soon.

Northside Lynch Mob Rules Forever!

Your fellow lyncher,
Taylor Ryan

10

"What's that?" Jesse Lee asked as he settled down on the overturned metal bucket that he had found in the creek behind the log cabin. Zoe-Linda and the twins sat in the middle of the cabin on an old army blanket they had brought from home. Dust danced in the sunlight that poured through the gaping hole in the roof.

Taylor followed Jesse's pointing finger. It was aimed at the small, black hangman's noose on his left shoulder. He had just taken off his shirt, it was so hot and stuffy inside the cabin.

"That's my tag," Taylor replied.

"You mean tattoo?"

"Yeah, sorta, but it's only permanent ink. I did it myself."

"What does it mean?"

"It means I belong to the Northside Lynch Mob."

"Lynch Mob? You don't really go around lynching people in the city, do you? I thought that went out with cattle rustling and horse thieving."

Taylor laughed. "You sure don't know much about living in the city, do you?"

Jesse scratched his head. "Nope, guess I don't. Don't reckon I'll ever be going to a big city, anyhow. So is that Lynch Mob a gang or something?"

"A gang? Shoot, no. Not exactly. We just hang out together. You know, after school and on weekends and during the summer. We don't rob banks or steal cars or stuff like that. We just mess around all day. Worst we ever did was snitch a few hubcaps."

"That's stealing, ain't it?"

"No, no. We weren't doing it for money. We were doing it for fun. It isn't stealing if you do it for fun, like say you snitch your baby sister's doll and hide it. That isn't stealing."

"She ain't got no dolls," Zoe-Linda chirped. "Last doll Vonda Sue had got throwed out the window by Lawrence here."

Lawrence looked up at Taylor with a missing-front-tooth grin.

"Landed smack dab in the middle of the Brazos River," Lawrence boasted.

Vonda Sue scooted away from her twin

brother, crossed her arms, and glared at him.

"Well, even if she did have a doll, why would I want to steal it from her and hide it?" Jesse said. "That'd make her bawl her eyes out for sure."

Taylor heaved a sigh. This guy was really dense.

"Okay, it's like this. This is the rule: When you take something for fun, it isn't stealing, it's snitching. When you take something so you can sell it and make a profit, then it's stealing. See?"

"Well, Zoe-Linda wasn't going to sell those bags of cornmeal, but you sure thought that was stealing."

Taylor ran his fingers through his hair. "Okay, she wasn't going to sell it, but she was going to *use* it. That's the same thing as selling it."

"All right then, I get it. If you take something to sell, or to use for yourself, then it's stealing. If you take something for fun, it's just snitching."

Taylor grinned. "Now you've got it."

"Who makes up them rules, anyhow?"

Taylor had to think a minute. It seemed that everyone just knew the rules without ever being told. He had to think hard to remember the first time he had snitched a candy bar. He didn't want to do it, but Jeremy said, "Watch me," and slid three Hershey's bars into the pocket of his baggy pants as fast as lightning and smooth as silk. "It isn't stealing," Jeremy had whispered, "it's just snitching. Mr. Hershey is a billionaire. He isn't going to miss a couple of candy bars. It only takes a penny for him to make one of these."

"I guess it was the leader of the Lynch Mob, Jeremy, who first told me the rules. But everybody knows them."

"Then, the way I see it," Jesse said slowly, "you stole them shells from the hardware store, because you sure planned to use them."

"Man, give me a break." Taylor plopped down on the floor and put his head in his hands. "Okay, okay. So the Lynch Mob *steals* now and then. Are you happy now?"

Jesse Lee picked up a piece of dried hay and stuck it in his mouth. He paused a long time before speaking.

"Ain't nothing 'bout stealing that makes me happy. I'm right sorry to hear that you belong to a gang that does such stuff. I thought you were a regular sort of guy. What else did that Lynch Mob leader teach you to do besides steal?"

Taylor jumped up. "Look, I told you we

don't call it stealing. If you're going to run down my friends, maybe we'd better forget about this whole reading thing. You never met Jeremy. He's a—a born leader. Like nobility or something. We have the reputation as the best gang in our neighborhood all because of Jeremy's leadership. He's like King Arthur and we're his knights at the Round Table."

Jesse Lee scratched his chin a minute, then tossed the twig away.

"I heard about that King Arthur. But I don't recall him telling his men to steal. Reckon maybe you're getting him mixed up with Robin Hood."

"Ma says Robin Hood was wrong stealing from the king's soldiers," Zoe-Linda quickly interjected. "She says even if Robin Hood didn't like the way the king was taxing the folks, him robbing the tax collectors was stealing just as much the tax collectors was stealing from the poor peasants. Ma's a real deep thinker, you know." Her bony fingers had twisted a long strand of hair around and around until it looked like red wire. "I heard that all gangs take dope. Did you ever smoke pot or take dope?"

Taylor laughed. But even as he said, "Of course not, silly," his mind fought back the image of DeWayne putting the plastic bag over his head and breathing in paint-remover fumes. In less than a heartbeat he had curled up on the ground, white foam specking his mouth, his eyes open and glazed over, his body jerking and twisting.

Taylor swallowed hard and tried to fight off the memory. But it came fast and clear now. He was running, running, following Jeremy and the others up the bayou embankment and down the street while DeWayne jerked into an immobile coma.

"Are you sick or something?" Zoe-Linda's voice broke into Taylor's thoughts.

"You're all sweaty and shaking," Jesse said. "What's wrong?"

Taylor shrugged and wiped his hand across his damp forehead. "Of course I'm sweating, it's about a hundred and twenty degrees in here." He walked outside, then sat on a big stump behind the log cabin. The Sinklers followed him and each one sat on a weathered gray stone slab. They may have been tombstones, but if so, the names of the dead had long, long ago faded away.

"Well, do you want to learn to read or what?"

The Sinklers all nodded. Taylor opened a

gunnysack and pulled out the ragged Dick and Jane books. He gave one to Jesse, one to Zoe-Linda, and the two little kids had to share one.

"Do you already know your ABC's?" Taylor asked.

" 'Course we do," Jesse protested. "We ain't stupid."

Taylor showed them each word while he read, then made them read. He also wrote each word in the dirt with a stick and had them repeat that word until they recognized it in the book. Zoe-Linda and the little ones caught on very fast, but Jesse struggled with each and every word.

"Why do those words all look scrambledy backwards to me?" he said in a voice full of frustration. "I ain't ever going to learn to read."

"Sure you can, Jesse Lee," Zoe-Linda said, putting her hand on his shoulder. "It's harder 'cause you're older. Ma always says bend a tree when it's a sapling and it'll grow the way you want it. You ain't a sapling anymore, so you'll just have to try harder than us. But you can do it. Remember what Ma always says about things coming too easy?"

Jesse nodded. "She says if things come too easy you don't appreciate them. That those who have to work for their bread enjoy it a lot more than those who get it free. Well, this ain't bread." He slammed the book closed and leaped to his feet. "I've got to go shoot some supper. You younguns go back home. Taylor, you coming with me to get your practice shooting in?"

Taylor hated to leave the kids with a half-finished lesson, but he knew Jesse was upset, so he said yes. They practiced shooting at tin cans, but Jesse wasn't very talkative. When they parted, Taylor half expected the tall redhead to say he didn't want to continue lessons.

"Will I see you tomorrow at the log cabin?" Taylor asked cautiously.

Jesse adjusted his hat. "I guess I knew it wouldn't be easy. Just struggling with them words brought back a lot of bad memories of kids laughing at me last time I was in school."

"I wasn't laughing. Your brother and sisters weren't laughing."

Jesse sighed. "All right. I'll give it another try. At least till the end of the week. I promise I won't squawk until then, no matter how much it hurts up here." He tapped his head. "Gotta go get supper or Pa will take his belt to my backside." He reached out and shook Taylor's hand. "Much obliged for your patience, Taylor," he said, then disappeared into the bushes. A few minutes later Taylor heard the sharp crack of the rifle and knew that another rabbit had bitten the dust.

He walked over to the bait house. It was Monday so there weren't as many pickups at the little motel. They wouldn't start arriving until Thursday or Friday. But there was a shiny new red double-cab Chevy pickup in the drive. A pot-bellied man with a clean white Stetson on his head stood under the shade of the big cottonwood tree, one fancy lizard-skin boot propped on the picnic table seat. Uncle Earl sat next to the boot, sipping a glass of iced tea.

Taylor couldn't hear everything the man was saying, but there was no doubt he wasn't very happy about something. And the way Uncle Earl was twitching was a lot like a school-boy being chewed out by the principal. Taylor walked up very quietly. No one seemed to notice him except Lecil, who popped the top off a bottle of Big Red strawberry soda and handed it to him. Taylor leaned up against the cotton-wood and listened.

"I know it's Vernon Sinkler," the big man said. "I heard the hounds barking late last night, way past midnight. This morning I drove to the lower forty, near the creek, and found a dozen post oak stumps. Cut close to the ground with an ax."

"Any clear evidence that it was Vernon?"

The man removed his expensive white Stetson and wiped a handkerchief across his sweaty brow.

"Nope. Even the tire tracks were in the grass, so they weren't very clear. Vernon is too smart to leave any evidence."

"If there's no proof, there's nothing we can do, Yancy. Now, I know Gideon hired him to thin out some land, and I hired him to thin out down by the creek. Maybe he just didn't realize he was on your land."

Yancy slammed his fist down on the picnic table. "Any fool knows where my land begins. I've got signs posted all over the place."

"It was only a few post oaks. Now, that's not going to kill you, is it? They probably needed thinning out."

Yancy's face turned red and he swatted his hat against his leg.

"Why are you standing up for that no-'count thief, Earl? Everybody knows Sinkler is a good-for-nothing poacher."

Uncle Earl shrugged. "I just don't believe in convicting a man without a trial. If you or anyone else catches Sinkler red-handed, that's a different story."

"Say what you will. I know he's the one. And I'll be waiting for him with a shotgun the next time." Yancy crammed his hat back on his head and stomped back to his shiny red Chevy. The tires spun and gravel spat as the truck tore across the parking lot.

Lecil, standing in the door of the general store, shook his head. The unlit cigarette moved up and down as he spoke.

"Yancy's always hated Sinkler."

"It appears to me that everyone around here hates Sinkler," Taylor said, then finished off the strawberry soft drink. Uncle Earl and Lecil both laughed.

"You could be right." Uncle Earl groaned as he lifted his tall frame from the picnic table and put his sweat-stained hat back on. "Well, Taylor, do you want a ride back up the mountain? Did you finish your business in the log cabin?"

Taylor felt heat creep up his neck.

"What do you mean, finish my business? I was just messing around the cabin. You know, learning more about my ancestors."

Lecil snorted and chuckled at the same time as he slapped a big catfish on a worktable attached to the side of the café. He slid a sharp gutting knife into the fish's soft underbelly and cleaned it so fast Taylor's eyes couldn't follow the movements. Then he brought a meat cleaver down and beheaded it with one stroke. Taylor often wondered how Lecil had killed his wife, but at times like this he didn't really want to know.

"Aunt Etta will be glad to hear you're interested in your ancestors," Uncle Earl said. "But don't get her started on the log cabin, though, or you'll regret it."

"Why?"

" 'Cause when Miss Etta's mouth gets cranked up, nothing can stop that motor," Lecil said. "I can still see her standing in front of the blackboard talking about that log cabin and the pioneers." Lecil grabbed another fish and gutted it. He quickly washed the fish, then wrapped them in a newspaper and handed them to Uncle Earl. "Tell Miss Etta she'd better give me an A-plus for these fish." His cigarette stuck out from his grinning lips.

"Thanks, Lecil. Drop on by for supper tomorrow."

As the yellow pickup grunted and rumbled up the mountain road, Taylor glanced at the rock chimney of the log cabin peeking through the dense shrubs and cedar trees. Earl looked in the same direction.

"A lot of history took place in that cabin," he said.

"How old is it?"

"Tobias Butler built it in 1848."

"Same time as he built the gristmill."

"Well, hey now, you *were* paying attention, weren't you? Well, ol' Tobias was no ordinary man. All he wanted to do was run his mill and have enough space for a cabin and a vegetable garden. He had three young sons and a wife back in Tennessee. His two brothers came with him to help build the mill and the log cabin. He sent for his wife and the boys when they finished. Tobias believed in live and let live. He was good friends with the Indians and never once took their land. His second wife was a Tonkawa princess."

"You mean I'm part Indian?" Taylor sat up and twisted in the seat. Uncle Earl held his hand up and shook his head.

"I said his *second* wife. Remember, you're descended from William Bradley, his youngest son by his first wife, Rebecca. William was born in that log cabin in 1850 and his mother died a few weeks later in that cabin."

Taylor shivered at the thought of someone

dying in the cabin where he had been sitting and messing around less than an hour ago.

"So, did Tobias have some children that were half-Tonkawa?"

"Nope. Unfortunately, his second wife didn't live long at all. She died real young, and so did his third wife."

"He had *three* wives?"

"Pioneer life was hard on women. Most of them died in childbirth or from exhaustion. Most of the babies died, too. Those headstones back behind the cabin are the graves of all of Tobias Butler's children. Nobody even knows all their names."

Taylor remembered the little black and gray stones behind the cabin, so worn that the names had been eroded away.

"So, if Tobias didn't take land from the Indians, how did you end up with Mockingbird Mountain?"

"The Tonkawa chief gave the mountain to Tobias as a gift because of his kindness toward his people. That was when Tobias was on up in years and the Indians were all being sent to reservations. The old chief said if the land had to go to white men, he wanted it to go to Tobias. Said Tobias was the only honest white man he'd ever known and respected. Farmers around here didn't care one way or another, since you can't grow crops on the mountain anyhow."

Taylor looked out the window at the dark cedars rolling past. Even though it was eight o'clock, it was still light enough to see a flash of red as a cardinal flew across the road. A few seconds later he heard the bird's loud chirping melody.

"Did all our relatives live in the log cabin?"

"Only till the 1880s. 'Bout that time, my grandfather, Jonathan Butler, built the stone house up on top of the mountain. He let the local farmers use the log cabin as a one-room schoolhouse until 1945. That's where I learned my three R's."

"Your what?"

"Reading, 'riting, and 'rithmetic." He broke out into song. *"Taught to the tune of a hickory stick.* Hee, hee. Got my first kiss down by the gristmill. And it wasn't Etta Mae. She was born and raised in Pandora. But her first teaching job was right there in that cabin."

Taylor smiled. How appropriate that the old cabin was once again being used as a school. His mind was deep in thoughts of schoolhouses when the pickup hit a deep hole and the rifle on the gun rack shifted, bumping his head.

"Sorry about that," Uncle Earl said. "I keep meaning to fix the rack. It's missing one of its brackets."

"I don't mind," Taylor said as he adjusted the rifle back into position. He ran his hand over the burled wood stock. "Is this a deer rifle?"

Uncle Earl chuckled. "Nope, son. That's a 30-30 shotgun. The one on the top rack is a .22."

"Why do you need two rifles?"

"The .22 is for little varmints like rabbits and squirrels. The shotgun is for birds far away, or something really big that comes up on you all of a sudden. A shotgun has hundreds of tiny little lead buckshot stuffed inside one cartridge; they scatter all over the place when you shoot. It only takes a few of those buckshot to bring down a bird. 'Course, if you shot something up close, the buckshot would be close together and they would blow the animal in half. You don't have to be very accurate with a shotgun. A .22 has only one piece of lead shot; you need to be a marksman to hit your target. Are you interested in learning to shoot a rifle?"

Taylor shrugged.

"I'd be happy to teach you. My eyesight isn't what it used to be, but I reckon I can still hit the broad side of a barn. Long as it isn't moving, that is." He chuckled.

An idea began formulating inside Taylor's mind. He had been searching the house for ammunition for days but had not located it yet. Now was the perfect opportunity to get Uncle Earl to tell him where it was hidden.

"Do you have any shotgun shells around the house?" Taylor asked, trying to keep his voice sounding like he couldn't care less.

"Sure. Lots of 'em."

"Could I see what they look like?"

"Of course. I'll show you as soon as we get to the house."

The pickup ground to a halt in front of the stone house. It was already dark and Aunt Etta's profile loomed through the living-room window. As usual, she was bent over some kind of knitting or crocheting. She didn't even glance up when she called out: "Wipe your feet."

"Yes, ma'am," Taylor said meekly, and scraped the bottoms of his shoes on the rough welcome mat. He followed Uncle Earl to his bedroom. It was the one place he had not thought to look.

The bed was one of those four-poster types

of dark mahogany wood—the kind that looked like George Washington would have slept there. A star pattern quilt covered the bed, and another quilt with round circles on it hung over a quilt stand. Uncle Earl opened the top drawer of a tall chest. Taylor shook his head in amazement. He never would have dreamed Uncle Earl kept his ammunition in a bedroom dresser drawer next to his underwear.

"Here, this is what a shotgun shell looks like. These little ones are .22 shells."

He held a three-inch red cylinder in one hand and some loose brass .22 cartridges in the other. Taylor smiled as he looked at the shiny brass shells.

"Thanks. I always wondered what a shotgun shell looked like."

"Well, how about it, Taylor? Want to do some target practice tomorrow after work?"

Taylor felt the temptation easing over his body. Here were hundreds of shells in the boxes. They could practice for hours without running out. And Uncle Earl would probably get a kick out of teaching him. Taylor almost said yes, but then he imagined Jesse Lee, sitting on the stump, struggling with the words in a Dick and Jane book. Without giving the rifle lessons, Jesse would no longer have an excuse to get reading lessons. Taylor turned away from the offering in Uncle Earl's hand.

"Naw," he said with a shrug. "Mom hates guns and told me to never touch one. I don't want to press my luck with her."

A wave of disappointment clouded Uncle Earl's blue eyes, but he didn't say anything. He gently replaced the bullets and closed the drawer.

"I don't blame her. I don't blame her one bit." He put his weathered hand on Taylor's back and steered him to the hallway.

As they walked into the living room and passed the photograph of his father, Taylor had an urge to ask Uncle Earl if he had known the young man in the picture very well. Taylor had to bite his lip to keep the words from coming out. In a way he wanted to know more, but in another way he didn't want to hear another story about another relative.

Still, he couldn't get his mind off his father that night as he lay in bed. His mom never did talk about him or the accident that killed him. Taylor didn't even know if the wound had been self-inflicted, or if it was a hunting buddy, or maybe a total stranger from across the field who had killed him. Had he been shot in the front, or the back, or the head?

Taylor shivered and pulled the sheet up higher. He closed his eyes and tried to push thoughts of his father out of his head. Slowly, the image of his father lying on the ground dying became the image of DeWayne lying on the ground. Soon that became the image of DeWayne's goofy father standing over his unconscious son, a sad look in his eyes.

Taylor threw back the covers and walked to the desk. He drew out a blank sheet of paper and grabbed a ballpoint pen.

Dear Mr. Lockhart,

You don't know me, but I know your son DeWayne. I'm real sorry what happened to him. I saw you on TV saying that DeWayne wasn't the type of boy who took drugs and inhaled fumes. I just wanted to say that you're right, he wasn't that kind of boy at all. I hope he gets well very soon.

Sincerely,
A friend

11

Jesse kept his word. For the next four days he came to the log cabin in the evening. He didn't say another thing about not being able to read or folks laughing at him. He struggled and struggled with every word, like "struggling with a grizzly bear," he would say. Zoe-Linda and the younger ones picked up reading very fast, and they worked with each other in perfect harmony. Jesse would get frustrated and sometimes had to get up and "go spit in the creek," he would get so mad. But he stuck with it.

On Friday, Jesse read his first completed sentence through without help. It was the sentence "Jane saw Spot run."

Zoe-Linda leaped up, threw her skinny arms around Jesse's neck, and smacked him with her big lips. He pushed her away, then the other two kids rolled all over him. Even his dog, Spotty, barked and licked his hand. Taylor tried not to make a big deal out of it, but he felt as good inside as if his home team had just won a big game. To celebrate, Taylor handed Zoe-Linda a five-dollar bill and asked her to go buy all of them a soft drink from Earl's General Store. She leaped to her feet and grabbed the two little ones before Jesse could protest.

"You oughtn't be giving her money like that, Taylor. She'll come to expect it of you and get all disappointed when you say no," Jesse said with a sigh.

Taylor shrugged. "I don't think so. She knows you earned it. Besides, I wanted to talk to you alone about something."

Jesse looked up from the book.

"Was it something Pa done?" he asked.

"No, nothing like that. I'm looking for advice, I guess you could say."

"Oh." A look of relief passed over Jesse's face. "About what?"

Taylor took a deep breath. "Well, it's something that happened to me back in the city. There was this guy, you see, and he used to follow me everywhere, you know, tagging along like a dog. Always wanting to do what I did and stuff like that. Do you know what I mean?"

Jesse snorted. "I surely do. Lawrence went

through a stage like that not more than two months ago. Couldn't shake him off with a stick."

"What did you do?"

"I took him aside one day and said, 'Looky here, Lawrence. You're my little brother and I love you dearly, but if I'd a wanted a dog with me, I'd a brung Spotty along, so back off and give me breathing room.' "

Taylor thought about it a minute, then shook his head. "A little brother is different. You more or less have to put up with him. This guy was my age. He wanted to be my friend, but I didn't want him tagging along everywhere."

"I never had any friends, on account of us always moving around so much. I don't think I'd turn somebody away that wanted to be my friend."

Taylor ran his fingers through his hair and stood up. He paced around the stump a few times, then twirled around.

"This guy was a pest. And he was goofy looking. Nobody else liked him. He was embarrassing me, don't you see?" Taylor didn't know why he was getting so irritated. He should have known Jesse wouldn't understand. Jesse was too much of a loner to know what it was like to belong to a gang like the Lynch

Mob. Suddenly he wished he had never started the conversation.

Taylor turned toward the general store, wishing Zoe-Linda and the kids would hurry up and get back.

"Well," Jesse said, closing the book, "I reckon if the guy was a pest, I'd tell him: 'Looky here, fella, I'm honored that you like me, but you're tagging after me like a pot-licking hound. Do you want to be my friend or my dog?' "

Taylor laughed. "Now why didn't I think of that?"

"Well, what did you do? Did you get rid of him?"

"What?"

"Well, I reckon you did something ornery to get rid of that pesky boy or you would have never wanted my advice."

Taylor forced a smile and laughed dryly.

"Of course not. What makes you say that? I came here to visit my aunt and uncle. That solved my problem."

"Then what happened to the pest?"

"He's—I don't know. I'm here and he's still there, as far as I know."

"If he really does want to be your friend, then all you have to do is tell him you're sorry and he'll forgive you for being ornery. He'll come back like a dog wagging its tail after it's been scolded. He'll—"

"Just drop it!" Taylor interrupted. "Can we get back to the lesson now?" Taylor snapped up a picture book and turned the pages so hard he tore a sheet. Jesse stared at him, his mouth slightly open, but he didn't speak again.

Zoe-Linda returned, beaming. She not only had a soft drink for everyone, but bags of potato chips and Fritos.

"You sure know how to stretch a dollar bill," Taylor said.

"Lecil gave us these here chips out of the kindness of his dear little heart. He's an angel in disguise, don't you think?"

"I like his tattoo. It moves like a snake," piped up Lawrence.

Taylor thought about telling them that Lecil murdered his wife and served fifteen years in the state pen, but decided not to burst their bubble, at least not today.

By the time they finished the lesson, it was dusk and the whippoorwills were already crying to each other in the woods.

The next day was Saturday and the mill was closed. Taylor received his pay of sixty dollars, and he hated to admit it, but the thought of going into the tiny town of Pandora made his heart sing with glee. Jesse had to work for his pa in town all day and wouldn't be able to come to the log cabin until the usual time, after supper.

In town, Taylor bought some more little books, ones with easy sentences and not as many pictures. He didn't want Jesse to be embarrassed by being seen with a kid's book all the time. He found three simple sports books. They did have some pictures, but the pictures were about baseball, football, and basketball. Taylor was proud of Jesse's progress and knew that what he needed most was some self-confidence and encouraging words.

Taylor saw the Greyhound pulling out of the bus stop, but this time he hardly gave it a second thought. On a sudden impulse, he bought a Barbie doll for Vonda Sue, a baseball glove for Lawrence, a tackle box for Jesse Lee, and a fancy fishing lure for Uncle Earl. At the farmers' market, he bought the pink butter dish for Aunt Etta. By the end of the day, all he had left of his two weeks of wages was a few dollars.

When Jesse and the kids didn't show up that evening after supper, a funny feeling crept into

Taylor's heart. To keep busy while waiting, he decided to tidy up around the cabin. He filled in some of the chinks in the wall with fresh mud. He pulled up weeds and briars around the cabin and the headstones and tried to make out some of the names on the gray slabs. When he glanced at his wristwatch, he saw that an hour had passed. Maybe they had forgotten. It was getting darker, so Taylor knew he couldn't stay much longer.

At last he sighed and hid the bag of toys up the chimney flue. He kicked a rock into the creek, then started down the narrow path that led to the mountain road. Suddenly he stopped.

"Is somebody there?" he called out.

"Taylor," a tiny voice cried.

Taylor ran back to the cabin and saw Zoe-Linda standing there, trembling. Mud covered her feet and legs, and some grass and twigs were lodged in her mop of red hair. Big tears rolled down her cheeks and past her quivering lips.

"What's wrong?" Taylor asked, surprised that his voice sounded so shaky.

"Pa whupped Jesse Lee real bad." She plopped down on the tree stump. Taylor squatted beside her.

"Why'd he do that?"

"He found out Jesse Lee used up some bullets for target practice. Pa said that was selfish and wasteful of Jesse, and he was going to take the price of bullets out of his hide."

Fury blazed through Taylor's blood like a wild fire.

"Didn't Jesse tell him that it was me who was target shooting?"

She shook her head and sobbed. "No, he didn't want you to get into trouble. He didn't tell Pa 'bout us learning to read, either. Jesse Lee said one person being beat up was enough. Oh, poor, poor Jesse Lee." She put her face in her hands and sobbed pitifully. Taylor put his arm around her skinny shoulders and squeezed.

"Don't worry, I'll help Jesse. I'll go to your pa and explain that it was me using up the bullets. I'll give your pa all my money. That should make him happy."

"You'd do that for Jesse Lee?"

"Sure, why not." Taylor shrugged, but inside his chest his heart was pounding at the mere thought of facing Vernon Sinkler's wrath. He looked like the type who would just as soon shoot a boy as look at one.

Taylor wiped Zoe-Linda's tears on his shirt-tail, then helped her to her feet. She smiled and hugged his neck so hard she almost choked him.

"Take me to where your trailer is," Taylor said.

"No, forget about Pa!" An angry voice came from the direction of the creek. Taylor twirled around and saw Jesse standing there, the rifle slung over one shoulder and a gunnysack over the other. His left cheek and eye were red and swollen and there was a cut on his chin.

"Jesse Lee! Does Pa know you went out?"

"Don't matter what Pa knows," Jesse said as he rested the rifle against the log cabin and swung the sack to the ground. He opened it and took out the cheap picture book about the three little pigs. "I've come for my reading lesson, Taylor. I'd be obliged if you'd finish teaching me how to read this story about the smart pigs. It's my favorite."

"Are you sure it's okay to be here?" Taylor asked. "I don't want you to get into any more trouble. I feel awful about using your bullets for target practice. I—I should have paid you for them."

Jesse held up a hand. "Aw, forget it. I don't care about Pa anymore. I've decided to get me an education, no matter what. I'm going to learn to read and write and go back to school. I don't want to ever end up like Pa. I'd rather be dead than live like him." He took off his cap and slammed it to the leaf-covered ground. "I don't care if I have to sit with little first-grade kids, I'm going back to school."

Zoe-Linda put her hand over her mouth to stifle a little cry.

"Zoe-Linda, it's getting dark. Go on back to the trailer before Ma starts looking for you."

"Aren't you coming with me?"

"Nope. I'm not coming back tonight. I brought a blanket to sleep on and a lantern. I'm going to stay here all night and read this book, if it's the last thing I do."

"That's a great idea," Taylor said. "I'll go get some stuff from the store and call my aunt and uncle and tell them I'm camping out."

Zoe-Linda reluctantly left, with warnings spewing from her lips.

"Pa will hunt you down and beat you again," she said, sniffing.

"Pa's got other things on his mind tonight," Jesse corrected her.

Taylor wasn't sure what he meant, but in the wee hours of the morning as he was just about to drift off to sleep, he heard the *tap-tap-tap* of an ax.

Jesse Lee looked up from the picture book he was hunched over. He turned toward the window, listened a minute, then glanced at Taylor, his dark eyes glimmering as the lantern light reflected off them. He sighed heavily, then turned back to the book. It was then that Taylor knew exactly where Vernon Sinkler was.

The next morning, Sunday, Jesse roused Taylor from a deep sleep.

"Thanks," Taylor said, rubbing his eyes. "Without Old Dixie to wake me up, I guess I would have slept all morning. And Aunt Etta will be spitting mad if I miss church." He grunted as Jesse gave him a hand up off the hard floor. His back ached and he had a crick in his neck.

"You can have all the food," Taylor said, pointing to a bag of potato chips, Oreo cookies, and a six-pack of Dr. Pepper.

"Much obliged, Taylor. If you don't mind, I'll stay here a spell."

"Sure, stay as long as you want. I'll try to come here again as soon as we get back from church, probably around two o'clock."

Taylor felt bad leaving Jesse all alone, but he knew the redhead could easily take care of himself. Besides, no one ever visited the log cabin. Even Uncle Earl admitted that he hadn't been there in over a year.

As Taylor walked out onto the mountain road, he waved to Lecil. All the short, muscular man had on was his boxer shorts and a sleeveless undershirt. Taylor could see the dragon tattoo all the way across the road. *Doesn't that man ever sleep?* he wondered as he trotted up the mountain path.

By the time Taylor reached the top, he was sweating and huffing and puffing. Only seven in the morning and already he was hot. He was famished, too, and couldn't wait to sink his teeth into some of Aunt Etta's homemade biscuits smothered with gravy. Or maybe today it would be pancakes piled high with melting butter and Aunt Jemima syrup, served with a glass of ice-cold milk.

But as Taylor swung around the corner of the rocky road and the flagstone house came into view, he stopped dead in his tracks.

"Oh, no," he moaned. In the drive was a familiar white Ford with a pink fuzzy ball attached to the tip of the antenna. Taylor knew that car very well. He had ridden in it a thousand times since he was a kid. It was his mother's car!

With a groan, Taylor remembered the letter he had written to her last Saturday. He knew exactly why she was there.

12

A feeling of panic and dread seized Taylor as he walked to the front steps of the stone house. While he scraped the dirt off his shoes out of habit, he heard his mother's voice inside the house and Uncle Earl's laughter.

Taylor turned the doorknob slowly and slipped through the door. Lucy growled until she saw it was him, then she wagged her tail and licked his hand. His mother was sitting at the kitchen table, wearing jeans and a short-sleeved pink blouse that matched a pink barrette in her curly dark hair.

"Hello, Taylor," she said in a voice that dripped icicles. She didn't even bother to stand up. She sipped a cup of coffee and finished up the last part of a plate of pancakes. From the aroma in the kitchen, Taylor knew that Aunt Etta had just baked fresh biscuits and scrambled some eggs, too. He was starving but didn't move. He just stood there in the middle of the living room, his life flashing before his eyes.

"Hi, Mom. What are you doing here?"

"Oh, I just thought I'd come and say good-bye to my only child before he gets his head shot off." She reached into her shirt pocket and took out the letter, then tossed it on the kitchen table. One thing about his mom, she never beat around the bush about anything. "What's this all about?" she demanded.

"Mom!" Taylor tried to put the right amount of whine and groan and indignation in his voice. "All I did was a little target practicing. Nobody got hurt."

Uncle Earl turned to Taylor, his eyebrows twisted in a puzzled expression.

"Thought you told me you didn't want to shoot the rifle," he said. Then he turned to his niece. "I told him I'd be happy to teach him, Virginia, but he wasn't interested."

Taylor watched the hurt look dragging down the corners of Uncle Earl's lips. He ran his fingers through his hair and shrugged.

"I didn't want to bother you, Uncle Earl. I was already getting instructions from someone." It wasn't exactly the truth, but then it wasn't exactly a lie, either. Taylor just didn't have the heart to tell the old man that getting instructions from a boy closer to his own age was more fun.

"Who's giving you instructions? Lecil?" Taylor's mother stood and the chair scraped across the linoleum floor. "I'll kick him to kingdom come, if he is."

"Now, Virginia, you know Lecil's parole doesn't allow him to own a gun."

"Yes, but I know you let him keep a shotgun in the back room."

"Just in case a varmint gets in the bait house. He hasn't had to use it but twice the past year. I think I know who's teaching Taylor. It's the Sinkler boy, isn't it?" Uncle Earl turned toward Taylor. "I see him now and then shooting rabbits."

Taylor felt the heat creep up his neck and flood over his face. He hung his head and nodded. "Yeah."

"Don't say, 'yeah,' to your uncle. Say, 'yes, sir,' " his mother insisted.

"Yes, sir." Taylor repeated her words without feeling.

"I sent you up here to get you away from hoodlums with guns, and now what do I find? You're not only hanging out with another hoodlum, he's teaching you how to shoot a gun!" She threw her hands in the air, then quickly lit up a cigarette. She had quit smoking about three years ago. She had to be really upset to start again.

"Jesse Lee isn't a hoodlum!" Taylor shouted. "He's hardworking and a hundred times more honest than me. He wouldn't even take the bullets I snitched for his rifle. You don't know him at all." Taylor didn't want to make her madder, but he couldn't stand by and let her talk about Jesse Lee like that.

"Snitching bullets? Oh, great, now you're stealing again."

"What kind of bullets?" Uncle Earl asked.

".22 shells."

"Hmm. You got them from Polk's Hardware, didn't you?"

Taylor nodded, unable to look the old man in the eyes.

"All you had to do was ask me. I have three unopened boxes in my chest of drawers." The friendliness had washed out of his voice.

Taylor wanted to explain that he was afraid that no one would want him to learn how to use a rifle, that no one would want him associating with Vernon Sinkler's son, but it was too late. Too late for explanations, too late for apologies. It was just one more foul-up by Taylor D. Ryan.

"See what I told you about?" Taylor's mother said to Uncle Earl. She blew smoke from her nostrils, then crushed the cigarette butt in her plate of pancake syrup.

Aunt Etta stared at the plate, her lips all quivery. She took a deep breath, then smiled.

"Come on over here and have some breakfast, Taylor. You must be starved after camping out all night. The biscuits are getting cold. I've got another jar of fresh red plum jelly. It's your favorite." She turned to her niece. "Taylor ate the whole jar that Suzy Polk gave me at Christmas. It came from that stretch of red plums that grow wild along Miller's Creek." Aunt Etta paused a minute. "Someone else I know used to love that jelly, too."

Taylor's mom stared at the jar of shimmering red jelly, then a tiny smile crept to the corners of her lips. She snorted.

"Suzy Polk! Is that old crow still alive? I figured she'd have gone on to meet her maker by now." She chuckled. "I remember the time I climbed up a plum tree to pick one. She nearly scared the daylights out of me and chased me with a rake. And the trees didn't even belong to her!"

Aunt Etta laughed. "Oh, yes, she's eighty-nine and still chasing kids out of the plum orchard. Why don't you sit back down and have some jelly on a biscuit?"

Something seemed to come over Taylor's mother. She looked at her son with glistening eyes. If Taylor hadn't known his no-nonsense, hard-as-nails mother better, he would have sworn that she was about to cry. She sniffed, then raked a napkin across her nose and sat down.

Taylor sat across from her and began to smear the red jelly over a buttered biscuit. His mother didn't say another word until he had finished breakfast. Her voice wasn't mad anymore.

"Taylor, I think you'd better come back home with me," she said in a soft, sad voice. "You know how I feel about guns, especially hunting guns . . ." Her voice trailed off and she looked out the picture window into the woods. Taylor knew she was thinking about his father. Maybe she had seen him all wounded and dying. Maybe she had been with him when he got hurt. He didn't know. She wouldn't talk to him about it.

Taylor felt sick. He preferred for his mom to be mad. Then it was easy to yell at her and stomp out of the room. But when she got all sad and quiet like this, all he felt was guilt. He heaved a long, ragged sigh. Maybe he was getting what he deserved. If he hadn't sent her the letter, she wouldn't be here now. Funny how a person's point of view could change so much in a week. Ten days ago he would have been singing and dancing at the idea of going back home. But now, it was the thought of leaving Jesse Lee and even pesky Zoe-Linda that made him feel empty inside.

Jesse needed him now, more than ever since running away from his pa. Taylor had to convince his mother to let him stay.

"Mom, if it's because of the rifle, don't worry, I don't target practice anymore. That was a whole week ago I wrote that letter. I was target practicing just to break up the boredom. Now I help Uncle Earl at the gristmill and Lecil at the bait house and grocery store. We go fishing all the time, don't we, Uncle Earl?" Taylor pleaded.

Uncle Earl scratched his chin a second, then nodded. "Yep, we sure do. Taylor caught three catfish last Monday. He's got a real gift for fishing, Taylor does. Don't know when he'd find time to be target practicing, do you, Etta Mae?"

Aunt Etta glanced at Uncle Earl and, as if a secret message had passed by telepathy, she nodded.

"Gracious, no. Taylor is too busy helping out with the donkeys and goats and chickens and other chores. He cleaned out the chicken coop just last Wednesday. He wouldn't have time to go gallivanting around the mountain shooting up tin cans. Not that I'd mind if he did."

Taylor's mother crossed her arms and pursed her lips as she looked first at Aunt Etta, then Uncle Earl.

"I know what you two are up to," she said. "You did the same thing for me when my mother would come to visit." She tapped her long, manicured nails against her arms a minute, then sighed heavily.

"Okay, okay. I can see I'm outnumbered today. But I'm warning you—all of you—that I don't want my son shooting guns, even if it is just target practice."

All three smiled and nodded.

"Ginny, why don't you come to church with us?" Aunt Etta said. "Brother Patterson would be pleased to see you again. Remember the time he gave you a big hug and your hair got caught in his suit button? You hollered like a stuck pig."

Taylor's mother ran her fingers through her short, curly hair.

"Yes, and that's one of the reasons I like to wear my hair short now. Thanks, but no thanks. I didn't bring a dress. Besides, I just came to get Taylor and run. I didn't intend to stay long. I guess I'll just head on back."

Aunt Etta walked across the room and put her arms around her niece's shoulders. "Honey, why don't you and Taylor stay here and visit while Earl and I are at church, then join us at the Rusty Corral for lunch. I'm sure the Good Lord will understand. Remember that place you and I used to visit? We called it our cathedral. It's just as good as a church. Maybe Taylor would like to see it."

Taylor watched his mother's eyes turn watery. She hugged Aunt Etta, then gave Uncle Earl a hug and slobbery kiss.

"You two are still the kindest people I know. I think I *will* show Taylor our cathedral."

Taylor was torn inside. Part of him was yelping with joy that he wouldn't have to sit through another Sunday sermon, but another part of him was apprehensive about being alone with his mother. She had a way of giving sermons of her own.

At first Taylor thought his mother didn't

know where she was going. He followed her on foot down the dirt road, then down a narrow goat trail flanked with tall grass and weeds. She marched right up to the edge of the mountain, narrowly missing a gigantic clump of prickly pear cactus covered with iridescent yellow blooms that attracted a horde of honey bees.

They stood on a large gray cliff that jutted out over the valley. She hadn't said a word all this time. Now she breathed in the pure, sweet air and her green eyes swept across the scene below—verdant fields of cotton and sorghum separated by isolated oak groves or barbed-wire fences. The bubbly clear water of Miller's Creek twisted and meandered over gray limestone boulders until it arrived at the river. And on the other side of the lazy river more green fields and pastures provided forage for grazing cattle and horses. On the nearest mountain, the tin roof of a farmhouse twinkled in the sun.

"It brings back a lot of memories," Taylor's mother said in a voice so soft that the wind swishing through the cedars almost carried it away.

"Is this what you call the cathedral?" It was the same cliff from which Taylor had first watched Jesse Lee shoot a rabbit.

She nodded. "Aunt Etta and I used to come up here to talk. Somehow, no matter what you say, it seems important and philosophical when you're on top of a cliff. Even if all you say is 'pass the peanut butter,' it seems profound. At least that's what Ted used to say."

"Ted?" Taylor's heart stopped, then started again about ten times faster. "You came up here with my father?"

She swallowed hard, then nodded. "It was our special place. We would sit and talk for hours. Sometimes we wouldn't say a word, just look out at the valley or into each other's eyes."

"I didn't know he—Ted—my father ever came here."

"He was born and raised in Butler's Hope. His family lived in one of those little houses at the foot of the mountain."

Taylor's astonishment left him speechless. There couldn't have been more than a dozen families on the mountain, and to think that his father had once been one of them.

"Were you raised in Butler's Hope, too?"

His mother shook her head, then cleared her throat.

"No, I wasn't. I was born and raised in Dallas. But we used to come visit here now and then. Once I stayed here the whole summer."

"Yeah? When?"

"When I was thirteen and full of stubbornness and thought I knew everything." She glanced at Taylor, then forced a smile and began walking again, fast. "Follow me, I want to show you something."

She walked right to the left edge of the rounded gray cliff and hung her legs over the side. Taylor thought she was going to jump, and a little noise slipped out of his mouth.

"This is an old Tonkawa Indian trail Ted told me about years ago," she called out. She waved him over closer to her. "This whole cliff is full of Tonkawa relics. See those round holes?" She pointed to several perfectly round holes in the cliff, most filled with water or mud and grass.

"Those are grinding holes. The women would put grain in there and grind them with stone pestles. Your father and I spent many a day looking for arrowheads and other artifacts. Found plenty of them, too."

"You? Digging in the dirt?"

Taylor's mom laughed for the first time that morning. "I guess it is hard to imagine. But I didn't always have long fingernails." She held up her slender fingers, each tipped with a perfectly manicured nail. With a squeal, she slid on her bottom over the cliff and disappeared into the treetops.

"Mom!" Taylor shouted and ran to the edge. She stood below, waving up at him.

"Just slide over the edge real gently and you'll land on this little spot of soft dirt. Hold on to that tree limb to your left."

Taylor grabbed the flimsy limb growing precariously out of the cliff and slid over the edge. He landed on the soft earth covered with about a million years worth of dead cedar leaves. The air was pungent with the odor of decaying leaves and sweet cedar.

"The Indians used this trail so many years, it's still here. Every now and then you can see a pattern in the stones or a tree bent over a certain way. Those were directional signs. Nowadays, the goats and the deer use the trail. And one or two curious kids like me and you."

She stooped over and crab-walked under some low tree branches until they were standing directly under the overhang of the cliff.

"Wow!" Taylor gasped as he saw the opening to a cave. "This must be where Lecil hid from the law." He started to crawl inside, but she grabbed his shirt.

"Not so fast. There's probably a nest of rattlesnakes in there. That's not what I wanted to show you anyway." She led him around the cliff to a far corner. It was very damp there and fuzzy green moss grew between seeping water. She pushed away dirt, debris, and overhanging tree limbs as if she were looking for something. As the minutes ticked, she grew more frustrated.

"It's got to be here," she groaned.

"What?"

She refused to answer. Suddenly she said "Yes!" and clawed at a clump of stubborn bindweeds. Her nails were getting chipped and broken. When she finally stood, she was out of breath and her face was flushed. Her once-neat hair had twigs and dirt lodged in it and was sticking out in all directions, but her voice was triumphant.

"Come look," she said.

Taylor crawled beside her and stared at the spot she had cleared away.

"TDR," he read the initials carved neatly into the stone. "Those are my initials."

"No, no. Those are your father's initials. Theodore David Ryan. And here are mine. VSB—Virginia Susan Butler—Ginny Sue.

That's what Ted always called me. He was your age when he carved these. I was only ten years old. I loved him even back then, but he didn't know it."

Taylor's mother sat down in the dirt and put her head in her hands. Taylor thought she was crying, so he sat next to her and felt miserable, not knowing what to do. When she looked up, her eyes were dry. She took in a deep breath and looked at him.

"I'm okay." She pushed Taylor's hair back with a dirty hand and smiled softly. "You look so much like him. Don't you see, Taylor, that's why I can't let you be around guns. If anything happened to you, Ted would never forgive me. And neither would I."

"You never told me how it happened—the accident, I mean."

His mother's face suddenly clouded over and then went pale. She shook her head.

"I can't."

"Why not? I'm not a little kid, Mom. I'm thirteen. I've seen movies and TV shows and pictures of people being killed. I can take it."

His mother's throat moved as she swallowed hard. "I'm glad to hear that, Taylor, but I'm not sure *I* can take it. It was so horrible."

Taylor glanced down at the ground and dug a hole in the soft humus with the toe of his sneaker.

"Mom . . . it was an accident, wasn't it? I mean, he wasn't murdered or anything like that, was he?"

"Of course not. He didn't have any enemies. Everyone loved Ted."

"Well, then did he kill himself? Was it suicide?"

"Your father would never commit suicide," she hissed. "He had his whole future ahead of him. He loved me, and he loved you. He was the happiest man on earth." She bit her lower lip to keep it from quivering.

"Then why won't you tell me what happened?" Taylor's voice rose with his impatience.

"I think it's time to go back." His mother stood and turned back to the path.

"It isn't fair, Mom. He was my father. I have the right to know. Was he shot in the back or in the chest or was it the head? What kind of gun was it? Was it a little .22 or was it a shotgun?" Taylor was shouting at his mother's back and he could see her shaking, but he didn't care. "Who shot my father?" he screamed.

His mother twirled around. Tears streaked down her cheeks.

"I did!" she yelled at the top of her lungs. "Oh, sweet Jesus, I shot him." She collapsed to her knees and sobbed.

Taylor felt all the blood drain from his face and the trees began to swirl around him. Suddenly he could not breathe.

"How?" he finally forced the word out, but it was hardly more than a whisper.

His mother sobbed, then drew in a deep breath.

"Ted loved hunting so much. He wanted me to learn, too. I went along because I loved him. We were turkey shooting in south Texas. I had just shot my first turkey and I was so excited I ran and picked it up. I was holding it in one hand and running back toward Ted, carrying the gun in the other. I was so excited I forgot to put the safety latch on." She paused and gasped for air. "He was so proud. His face was beaming with love and he was clapping. Just before I reached him, I stumbled and fell. The gun went off and shot him in the heart." She put her face in her hands and shook her head, as if trying to shake away the memory. "I'm so sorry, Taylor. I took away your father and ruined your life. I don't blame you for hating me."

Taylor put his hand on her back, then

wrapped his arms around her neck and kissed her forehead. It took all the strength he could muster to keep from sobbing along with her.

"I don't hate you, Mom. It was an accident."

She lifted her face and sniffed. "I just couldn't tell you. All these years I've kept it buried inside because I didn't think you would understand."

"I understand, Mom. I really do." He took her elbow and helped her up from the ground. She hugged him with all her might, then wiped her runny nose, leaving streaks of mud across her face. She laughed lightly.

"I must look a mess," she said, holding up her broken nails and dirty hands. They started back up the cliff, which was considerably more difficult than getting down it. At one point, his mother paused and pointed to some scratching on the underside of the gray cliff.

"Those are the initials of every boy in Butler's Hope for the past hundred and fifty years. It's like a male ritual or something. They camp out in the cave, rattlesnakes and all, and then carve their initials here. Let's see if we recognize any. Yeah, there's my dad's—WWB—oh, and look, there's Uncle Earl's initials—HEB. His middle name is Earl. He hates his first name."

"What?"

"He'd kill me if I told you." She leaned over and whispered, "Horatio," then giggled. "This is the oldest one—TJB—Tobias Jackson Butler—1850. And, of course, here's your father's initials again." Her fingers caressed the letters. "Maybe you'll carve your initials before you leave."

"I think I will," Taylor said, and gave his mother a hand up over the last few inches of cliff.

They got back to the stone house and cleaned up, then drove into town just in time to meet Aunt Etta and Uncle Earl at the Rusty Corral for lunch.

Just before she left, Taylor's mother opened her purse and took out a letter.

"I probably shouldn't show this to you," she said, "considering who it's from, but I'm not going to start censoring your mail." She held out the envelope and Taylor took it eagerly. He recognized the small, tight handwriting right away and the Arizona return address. It was from Jeremy.

"Thanks, Mom," he said, and hugged her a final time.

"I'll see you in a month," she said as she started her car.

Taylor couldn't wait to rip open the letter, but he resisted until he was safe inside his attic room and the door was locked.

Dear Taylor,

Tough luck being stuck on a mountaintop in the middle of nowhere. Man, it's hot here—104 yesterday, but my dad has a hundred-foot swimming pool that helps take care of the heat. And his servant, Maria, is a babe. She's been sneaking me marijuana every night. And she's hot!

About that jerk DeWayne. Don't worry your pretty little head. All that stuff that happened wasn't our fault. DeWayne should have told us he was allergic to paint remover. For Pete's sake, how stupid can you get, sniffing fumes of something that could kill you? And don't tell anyone what happened. You're only thirteen, they probably wouldn't do anything to you, but I'm sixteen now and could be sent to jail for life. Not that we did anything wrong. The best thing we can do is keep our mouths shut and pray that the geek kicks the bucket. I hear that he's not expected to live through the end of the week. Like they say, dead men tell no tales.

Gotta go. Maria is calling. Remember our motto: Friends before Family. I'm counting on you, Taylor.

Northside Lynch Mob Rules Forever!

Jeremy, the Jerm

A sickening feeling crept into Taylor's stomach as he put the letter down. He reread it two more times, then tore it into tiny little pieces, wrapped the scraps in another sheet of paper, then wadded that into a ball. He wasn't going to take any chances that Aunt Etta might read it.

Taylor turned off the light and crawled into bed, but all he could think about was DeWayne lying in the hospital bed, tubes running from his nose and needles in his veins. A great nausea churned in the pit of his stomach. Even the sound of hounds barking and the tap of the ax in the woods could not make him get up to write his daily letter. Besides, there was no one left to write to—no one but DeWayne himself.

13

Taylor wasn't hungry the next morning, but he sneaked some biscuits with sausage inside them to take to Jesse. He didn't feel like talking to Uncle Earl, so he told him he wanted to walk to the mill for the exercise. He hadn't even changed clothes and now they looked like a wrinkled mess. The old couple exchanged glances but didn't comment.

"I'll send your lunch with Earl," Aunt Etta said.

The cool morning air bristled with a blending of cedar, wildflowers, and earth dampened by an early morning shower. Clouds still hovered over the mountain, making it cooler than usual. Mourning doves cooed on the telephone lines and a lone mockingbird sang a refrain that lasted five minutes without a break. Cardinals darted across the road with no regard for humans, and a flock of crows shouted out disrespectfully from the branches of a dead cottonwood tree.

Taylor's eyes burned from lack of sleep, and

even the fresh morning air could not sweep away the cobwebs in his brain. He felt as if a motor in his head had been left on all night and was now overheated and smelling like burning oil.

By the time he reached the foot of the mountain, sweat had soaked through the back of his shirt. Uncle Earl's yellow pickup was in front of the grocery store, having arrived from the direction of the scenic route. He and Lecil were sitting at the picnic table under the cottonwood tree sipping coffee.

Taylor turned off the road onto the trail that led to the log cabin. He peeked through the window and saw Jesse Lee sitting on a bedroll, studying the "Three Little Pigs" book. When Taylor stepped on a twig, Jesse nearly jumped out of his skin and grabbed his rifle.

"Hold on!" Taylor shouted. "It's me."

Jesse leaned the rifle against the fireplace mantel.

"Well, now, don't you look like something that the cat dragged in. I haven't seen such red eyes since the last time my pa was out all night stomping at Lost Man's Saloon."

Taylor shrugged and handed him the biscuits and sausage.

"I couldn't sleep. Had a lot on my mind."

Jesse nodded toward the biscuits. "Mighty obliged, but you don't have to fetch food for me. I can provide for myself."

"Just take it, Jesse Lee. For once in your life, don't feel so obliged when somebody gives you something." Taylor plopped down on the overturned bucket and put his head in his hands.

Jesse sat on the floor and ate the food slowly.

"Something happen to you yesterday, Taylor? I kinda expected to see you later in the day."

Taylor didn't lift his head. "My mom was waiting when I got to the house. She drove all the way from Houston because she found out I was learning how to shoot a gun. She hates guns like you wouldn't believe." Taylor glanced over at the rifle leaning against the wall. His fingers itched to feel the warm wood and cold steel. "I won't be target practicing with you anymore. Sorry."

Jesse rose slowly. "Oh," he said in a voice heavy with disappointment. "Then I guess our reading lessons are done with."

Taylor jerked his head up. "No, no. I'll keep on teaching you and the kids. Don't worry about that." He saw Jesse open his mouth to protest. "I like teaching you. It's really lonely up here with no one my age to talk to."

"Maybe so, but it ain't right to take something for nothing. I've gotta pay you somehow."

Taylor stood up, heat rising to his face. "You're my friend, Jesse Lee Sinkler. And I want to teach you. Isn't that enough reason? Why do you always have to feel so obliged to everyone?"

"I was brought up that a man always pays his way."

Taylor's hands formed tight fists.

"Well, that isn't what I heard. I heard your pa steals post trees off of everyone's land. He doesn't *snitch* them, he *steals* them."

Jesse's face turned crimson under the tan and his Adam's apple bobbed as he swallowed hard.

"I ain't like my pa, and I don't intend to ever be. I had hoped that you realized that by now. But maybe I was just fooling myself." He picked up his old, crumpled cap and crammed it on his head, then grabbed the rifle and walked out the door.

Taylor knew that calling out would do no good and his patience had run out, so he just turned around and walked to the bait house and grocery store. Uncle Earl and Lecil watched him approach but kept on chatting. Taylor opened the ice bin and took out a cold cola. It wasn't very nourishing, but he needed some caffeine to give him some pep.

It was one of the longest mornings of Taylor's life. It reminded him of school mornings after staying up late with Jeremy and the gang. At least he was moving around a lot at the gristmill, loading grain, lifting bags. At lunchtime, after eating the sandwich that Aunt Etta had fixed, Taylor lay down on the cot under the cottonwood tree and fell into a deep sleep.

He woke with Elvis licking his hand. He sat up, rubbing his eyes and noticing that the sun was hanging low over the tops of the trees, barely visible through the clouds.

"Shoot!" he said, and leaped up. He ran to the gristmill and arrived just as Uncle Earl was locking up.

"I'm sorry," Taylor started to apologize, but Uncle Earl held up his hand.

"Don't worry about it," Earl said as he walked with Taylor back to the bait house. "Every man has a restless night once in a while. It was a light day at the mill anyhow. I'm going fishing. I want to try out that new lure you gave me. Fishing is always good before a rain. Maybe my streak of bad luck will break today. How about it?"

Taylor glanced at his watch. He wondered if Jesse Lee had told Zoe-Linda and the twins about their argument. He had the urge to find the Sinkler trailer and apologize to Jesse.

"I'd rather just explore around the mountain. I'm afraid I'd fall asleep again if I tried fishing."

Uncle Earl laughed. "Ain't that a fact. I'll probably be snoring away myself in thirty minutes. If I don't get home by dark, better come and drag the river for my body." He laughed again as he dipped a net into the minnow tank and put five squirming minnows with red tails into the minnow bucket. He repeated the process two more times until the bucket had a dozen tiny fish darting about and bumping against the metal sides.

Uncle Earl snapped the lid down and loaded the bucket into the back of the pickup.

"You want Elvis to go with you?"

Taylor shook his head. "No, you can take him. I'll be okay."

"He'd rather go with you. A boy needs a dog to keep him company, I always say. An old man like me just needs a fishing pole. And a cot."

Taylor glanced at the beagle's bright eyes and wagging tail.

"Okay." He whistled lightly and Elvis leaped from the pickup bed into his arms. Taylor caught him with a grunt and a laugh. The hound licked his face in appreciation.

Uncle Earl rubbed the dog's head, then climbed into the pickup. He paused before closing the door.

"Taylor, about what your mom said yesterday. I know you've been target practicing with Vernon Sinkler's boy . . ."

Taylor felt his heart do a flip-flop. "Don't worry, I won't do it anymore. I already told Jesse Lee."

Uncle Earl adjusted his weathered hat. "All right, then. It's not my place to tell Virginia how to raise her boy. But if I hear you target practicing, I'm not going to say anything to her. If you get my drift."

"I understand, Uncle Earl. Thanks, but like I said, I'm not going to use the rifle again. Jesse Lee got into trouble with his pa because of it. That's why I have to stop." Maybe he'd said too much, but Uncle Earl nodded like he understood what that meant. He adjusted his hat and drove away down the bottom road that led to the river.

When Taylor arrived at the log cabin, Zoe-Linda and the twins were already waiting. She was going over a Jack-and-the-Beanstalk picture book, patiently pointing out each word and having the kids repeat, just like Taylor always did.

"Hey, Taylor," she said, looking up.

Taylor glanced around.

"I guess Jesse isn't coming."

"I figured he'd be here," she said, petting Elvis on the head. "We haven't seen him since yesterday morning when he run away. Maybe he's out getting something to eat. I hate to admit it, but I miss those old greasy rabbits and squirrels. All we had last night was red beans and corn bread and green onions. Mama loves those green onions. She grows them in pots. Once when the trailer hit a big bump, the pots fell and broke. Mama cried like a baby."

Taylor wasn't in the mood for one of Zoe-Linda's mama stories, so he started the lesson right away. They were halfway through it when Jesse Lee stepped through the door, a limp rabbit hanging from his belt.

"I brung you a rabbit for supper," he said to his sister, dropping the body to the floor. She jumped up and hugged his neck. Each twin hugged one of his legs.

"I ain't been gone that long," he said, and gently pushed them all away. "Am I too late for the reading lesson?" he asked Taylor.

Taylor shook his head and tried to hide his

smile. "We were just getting to your favorite part of 'The Three Little Pigs.'"

"You mean where they boil the big bad wolf?"

"Yep."

Jesse flashed one of his very rare smiles, revealing teeth that could have stood a little bracing up. He settled on the blanket on the floor and took the book. In his usual singsong, determined voice he read the story from the beginning.

An hour later, Zoe-Linda gathered the kids and picked up the rabbit.

"You coming home, Jesse Lee? Pa swears he won't beat you no more."

"Nope. I ain't coming back."

"Pa says he's about finished around here. He's just got one more stand of cedars to cut to make a truckload. We'll be leaving tomorrow at daybreak."

"Thanks for the information, Zoe-Linda. Now get on home before dark. I don't want you to get whupped, too."

"Wait a minute," Taylor called out to the kids. He reached inside the chimney where he had stuffed the bag of toys. He handed Vonda Sue the Barbie doll, Lawrence the baseball glove, and Zoe-Linda a fancy picture book about a redheaded girl. They squealed with delight and Zoe-Linda wrapped her arms around Taylor and planted a slurpy kiss on his cheek.

"Now they're spoiled rotten," Jesse muttered. "And it ain't even Christmas."

"It's just going-away presents," Taylor said, shuffling his feet and feeling awkward. "You're leaving tomorrow and, well, I just wanted you to have something to remember me, that's all. It's nothing special."

"Taylor Ryan, I love you," Zoe-Linda shouted as she herded the children out the door. "And I'm gonna marry you someday."

After the children left, Taylor got up. "It's getting dark, I've got to get on back, too." He paused, searching for the right words. He sure didn't want to make Jesse get all huffy and mad again.

"Jesse, I'm glad you came back. I'm sorry for all those things I said about your pa. I don't even know the man."

Jesse shook his head.

"No need to apologize, Taylor. Everything you've ever heard about Vernon Sinkler is true. He's not much of a man. He hates people and hates learning. But I made a decision this morning walking around the mountain. I went up to that big gray cliff that looks across the fields and the river. You know the one I mean?"

"Yeah, we call it the cathedral."

"That's the one. Well, I made me a decision right then and there."

"What was it?"

"I decided I had me a choice: I could be stubborn and refuse to come back here for my lesson. I might end up exactly like my pa, with no education and no good job. Or I might face the fact that you are my friend and are offering to teach me in friendship and not expecting anything in return. I thought long and hard. And I don't mind telling you, swallowing my pride felt like swallowing a big jaggedy rock. But sometimes you have to swallow things that hurt, so I done it. And here I am. I don't want to end up like my pa."

Taylor held out his hand and they shook on it. Then he gave Jesse the tackle box. As expected, Jesse refused it, so Taylor put it beside the fireplace.

Taylor left Jesse that night hunched over the picture books, mumbling the words by the light of a coal-oil lantern.

Uncle Earl's yellow pickup was already in the driveway when Taylor arrived at the house. The smell of fried catfish drifted through the opened kitchen window. Uncle Earl's streak of bad luck had finally ended. So had Jesse's. Maybe it was time for Taylor's to end, too.

About four o'clock in the morning a loud ruckus roused Taylor out of a deep sleep. He rubbed his eyes and staggered to the window. He saw the sheriff's car, Mr. Yancy's flashy red Chevy, and two other pickups, all with their headlights on. Uncle Earl stood at the front door wearing his pajamas. The voices rose in anger and hounds yelped from the back of the trucks.

Taylor jumped into his clothes and ran down the stairs just as Uncle Earl hurried inside to change clothes.

"What is it, Earl?" Aunt Etta asked.

"They've got a posse up after Vernon Sinkler. Yancy swears he's going to blow Sinkler to kingdom come for cutting down his trees."

14

Taylor jerked on his sneakers and charged out the back door while Uncle Earl was still getting dressed. He flew down the mountain and reached the log cabin. Jesse was already awake, hunched over the picture books just like Taylor had left him. He looked up, his eyes round with surprise.

"Why, Taylor, you're up mighty early . . ."

"Jesse!" Taylor gasped for air and held onto the fireplace mantel. "The sheriff and his posse are looking for your pa. Yancy found his trees cut down last night and he says he's going to prosecute your pa."

The color drained from Jesse's face. "That derned fool. I knew he would get into trouble this time." Jesse grabbed his rifle.

"Where are you going?"

"I've gotta warn Pa."

"I thought you hated him."

Jesse sighed. "I despise him, but I can't let Pa go to prison. What would happen to Mama and the kids?"

"Well, after you warn him, are you coming back?"

"Nope, I reckon the sheriff considers me just another no-'count post cutter like my pa." He heaved a sigh, then crammed his cap over his red hair.

Taylor felt a sinking feeling. "I'll tell them you didn't have anything to do with stealing Yancy's posts. You were here all night."

"Wouldn't do no good."

"Well, you . . . you can hide here in the cabin the rest of the summer. I'll keep on teaching you to read and write. Maybe you could come live with me in Houston and go to school." Taylor felt pressure building up in his throat until he couldn't talk anymore.

Jesse Lee shook his head. "My family's in trouble. I've gotta put them first." He gathered up his blanket and lantern.

"What about me?" Taylor exploded. "I thought we were friends, Jesse! Friends come first, don't they?"

Jesse paused, then turned to Taylor. "Taylor Ryan, you are the best friend I've ever had, and I want to stay here more than anything else in the world. But sometimes you have to follow what you know is right in your heart. Now, I know Zoe-Linda and the twins can be real pesky, but they're my family and I can't let anything happen to them."

"But you're not going back to your pa, are you? He'll beat you up."

Jesse shrugged. "It don't matter. I know what I have to do from now on, and this is just one tiny little hill to get over." He picked up the picture book and handed it to Taylor gently. "Much obliged for loaning me the book."

"Take it. I have no use for it now." Taylor scribbled his name and address inside the book. He shoved it and the new tackle box into Jesse's hands. "Take these or else I'll punch you out. No arguing."

Jesse reached into his pocket and took out a very old, beat-up pocketknife.

"I'll take them if you'll take this. It ain't much, just an old skinning knife, but it's all I got."

"I'd be very honored to have it," Taylor said, smiling. They shook hands, then Jesse took off through the woods, clinging to the picture book and the new tackle box. Not five minutes later, Taylor heard the sound of a motor starting up and the rumble of the flatbed truck. Taylor cut through the woods to the main dirt road and looked through the trees in time to see the dark form of the truck and trailer bumping over a pasture, the headlights off.

Taylor watched until the truck had eased onto the main road and disappeared over the hill. The headlights never came on.

"Good-bye, Jesse," Taylor whispered to the wind. "I hope you know what you're doing."

By the time Taylor walked through the woods to the bait house and grocery store, the eastern sky was turning pink. Taylor heard Old Dixie crowing from the mountaintop and Lecil's rooster answering from his little shack. Lecil had opened up the café and the sheriff and posse sat under the cottonwood tree sipping coffee and chatting. The hounds bayed and circled around the store, their noses to the ground, but the men ignored them.

"What happened?" Taylor asked Lecil.

"Yancy started a ruckus and got his hounds after Vernon Sinkler, but old Vernon snuck away in the dark, as usual. He's as sly as a fox. Always knows when the getting's good. Learned that in the army, just like me." The cigarette bobbed up and down as he spoke. Then he grinned, revealing yellowed teeth.

"What do you mean, 'as usual'? Has this happened before?"

"About every year. Vernon slips in, Yancy gets mad and sics the hounds after him. Like the eternal ebb and flow of the tide, life goes on." He shrugged.

Taylor didn't see Jesse Lee again and didn't know if the tall redhead had left in the truck with his pa or if he had hitched a ride into town and struck out on his own.

That evening after supper, Taylor wandered aimlessly on the mountain. He carved his initials into the cliff, then, out of habit, walked down to the log cabin and sat on the overturned bucket. Deep loneliness wrapped itself around him as he took a Dick and Jane book out of the gunnysack full of school supplies stashed in the corner. As he idly flipped through the pages, he relived the past two weeks, from the moment he had first seen Jesse on the back of the flatbed truck to the last time he had seen Jesse running through the cedar trees. He thought about pesky Zoe-Linda and the sweet-faced twins and how they all stuck up for each other.

Taylor removed some paper and a pencil from the sack. He began writing, and as he wrote the words, a big lump came to his throat. He knew exactly what Jesse had meant by "swallowing a jaggedy rock."

Dear Jeremy,

Received your letter. Sounds like you've got it made, with the pool and maid and all. This letter is hard to write, but here goes. I've decided what you did—what we all did—to DeWayne was wrong. No matter how nerdy he is, it isn't right to wish him dead. I'm dropping out of the Northside Lynch Mob forever.

Sincerely,
Taylor Ryan

After folding the letter to Jeremy and stuffing it in his shirt pocket, Taylor took another sheet of paper from the gunnysack. He poised the pencil over the paper and waited for the right words to come. Outside the window, a gentle rain began to fall. The wind swished through the cedar trees until it sounded like someone whispering. In the woods, a whippoorwill cried to its mate. Taylor drew in a deep, deep breath and the words flowed onto the paper.

Dear Mom,

I am ready to come home. I want you to tell me everything about my father. And I have something to tell you, too.

There was this kid named DeWayne Lockhart and he wanted to be a part of our gang so Jeremy made him go through some initiation steps. Everything that happened is in a letter that I wrote and hid inside Dad's model airplane hanging above my bed. Don't worry, I'm not going to kill myself, that would be the coward's way out. Please read that letter and then do what you have to. I don't know if I'll go to prison or juvenile detention or what, but I know that what I did was wrong and I have to face whatever happens.

Love,
Taylor

It was the hardest letter Taylor had ever written. His heart pounded against his ribs and his fingers shook, but he stuck it out until the end. By the time Taylor finished the letter, his face was wet with tears.

Just as he expected, his mom came to pick him up the next Saturday. He said good-bye to the old couple, with tears flowing all over the place. Aunt Etta stuffed cookies and jars of jam into his duffel bag, and Uncle Earl gave him one of his lucky fishing rods. Lecil made him a stack of barbecue sandwiches and a jar of potato salad for the long drive back to Houston.

Taylor's mother had told the authorities about what happened to DeWayne. They were waiting for Taylor when he got home and gave him the fifth degree.

Taylor was in big trouble, but he knew he had to swallow the jaggedy rock and face his punishment. He was relieved that it was over. His mother took off work and attended the hearing. Taylor didn't have to go to juvenile detention but was put on probation and had to do community service. He chose to work at a literacy center, teaching teens how to read. And not a minute of it went by that he didn't think of Jesse Lee, Zoe-Linda, and the twins.

The day after he arrived home, Taylor took a city bus to the hospital. Taylor's stomach felt like it was tied in a knot as he walked down the long corridor. The smell of alcohol and medicine and sickness permeated his brain until he wanted to throw up.

DeWayne didn't have any tubes hooked up to his body. He lay very still and very peaceful. His eyes were open and he looked funny without his glasses, so Taylor slipped them over his nose. The chubby hand, once covered with freckles, looked pale now.

"I'm sorry, man," Taylor whispered as he took DeWayne's hand into his own. "I never meant for this to happen. It was just a stupid initiation trick. You didn't deserve this." Taylor paused to swallow down the jaggedy rock again. "I'm going to visit you every day. And I'll be here when you wake up."

Taylor felt a little twitch in DeWayne's hand, even though his face didn't move. That twitch was enough for Taylor. He said good-bye and promised to come again.

That was in late June. Taylor kept his promise and rode the bus to the hospital every day. One Monday in late August, after he got off the city bus and walked to his apartment, he found a letter addressed to him mixed in with the mail.

It had no return address and Taylor didn't recognize the childish handwriting. He ripped it open. It smelled like cedar.

Dear Taylor Ryan,

Bet you never thout you'd heer from yor old friend Jesse Lee. Ha, ha! Pa got away from the sherrif. He beat me up and I run away agin. I got a uncle in Fort Worth I run to. I got a day job. I go to school at nite. Gone to get my high school deploma someday. And it's all because of you being my friend. Thanks. Someday maybe we'll meet agin.

> Your little piggy friend,
> Jesse Lee Sinkler

Taylor read the letter three more times, folded it neatly, and slid it into his dresser drawer next to the skinning knife. He could think of nothing he'd like to do more than meet Jesse Lee again someday.